**'Then wha[...]
want, Da[...]**

'I don't want [...]
came closer, s[...] reached
out without ha[...] hold of her wrist,
pulling her inex[...]bly back towards him.

'Don't you?' he asked softly. His other hand
cupped her chin and his thumb stroked the line
of her jaw. 'Are you sure?'

Dear Reader

The first few months of a new year are a time for looking forward and wondering what the future holds for us. There are no such worries when you pick up a Mills & Boon story, though—you're guaranteed to find an exciting, heart-warming romance! This month, as usual, we've got some real treats in store for you. So, whatever 1995 brings you, you can be sure of one thing: if you're reading Mills & Boon, it's going to be a year of romance!

The Editor

Jessica Hart had a haphazard career before she began writing to finance a degree in history. Her experience ranged from waitress, theatre production assistant and outback cook to newsdesk secretary, expedition PA and English teacher, and she has worked in countries as different as France and Indonesia, Australia and Cameroon. She now lives in the North of England, where her hobbies are limited to eating and drinking and travelling when she can, preferably to places where she'll find good food or desert or tropical rain.

Recent titles by the same author:

LOVE'S LABYRINTH
THE RIGHT KIND OF MAN

PARTNER
FOR LOVE

BY

JESSICA HART

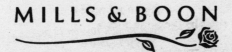

MILLS & BOON LIMITED
ETON HOUSE, 18-24 PARADISE ROAD
RICHMOND, SURREY TW9 1SR

All the characters in this book have no existence outside the imagination of the Author, and have no relation whatsoever to anyone bearing the same name or names. They are not even distantly inspired by any individual known or unknown to the Author, and all the incidents are pure invention.

First published in Great Britain 1995 by Mills & Boon Limited

© Jessica Hart 1995

Australian copyright 1995   Philippine copyright 1995 This edition 1995

ISBN 0 263 78894 6

Set in Times Roman 10½ on 12 pt. 01-9503-52686 C

Made and printed in Great Britain

CHAPTER ONE

DARCY stood under her umbrella and lifted her feet in turn to inspect her shoes with a grimace. She could remember Uncle Bill boasting that Bindaburra was in the driest part of the driest state in the driest continent in the world, but after two days of rain Darcy was beginning to wonder if he had been pulling her leg. The Australian outback was supposed to be hot and parched, not cold and wet and extremely muddy.

Scraping her shoes against each other gingerly to remove the huge clods of mud that kept gathering around them, Darcy looked around her, profoundly unimpressed by the spindly gum trees that lined the track and the low, sparse scrub stretching interminably off towards the horizon. Although there was still nearly an hour to go before dark, the rain had cast a dull pall over everything. Had she come all the way from London just for *this*?

Darcy sighed and continued trudging along the track. It was like walking through concrete. Every time she put one foot in front of the other, she had to drag it up through the mud, half of which stayed clogged around her shoes until they were so heavy, she had to stop and knock it all off again. She just hoped Bindaburra wouldn't be much further. She had been driving all day along slippery mud tracks like this one and she was tired and fed up. Why couldn't the car have managed a few minutes more instead of getting bogged frustratingly close to her goal?

Just then the sound of a vehicle changing gear as it approached the creek made her dark blue eyes brighten with hope. Surely whoever it was would be able to give her a lift for the last mile or so? Tightening her grip on her umbrella, Darcy picked her way cautiously into the middle of the track and got ready to wave enthusiastically.

It seemed a long time before the engine growled out of the creek and the vehicle accelerated towards her, its headlights boring through the gloom. Darcy, swinging the umbrella around, was transfixed by the powerful beams, a slim, incongruously vivid figure in the inhospitable landscape.

For one awful moment she thought that the driver hadn't seen her. Screwing up her eyes against the rapidly approaching light, she flapped her free arm frantically as she staggered out of the way.

To her relief, the car was slowing until she could see that it wasn't a car at all but a mud-splattered ute. Hardly the most glamorous of vehicles to be rescued by, thought Darcy, but since she hadn't seen another car for the last three hours she supposed she should be grateful it had come along at all.

The ute came to a halt beside her and the driver wound down the window as Darcy slithered towards it. The mud was so thick and slippery that she almost lost her footing and had to make a grab for the door to steady herself.

Slightly breathless but relieved still to be upright, she looked down into the cab with a winning smile. 'Hello,' she said, quite unconscious that her English accent was as incongruous out here as her appearance.

Her first thought was that the driver looked rather unfriendly. He had leant his elbow out of the window and was frowning at her with a mixture of exasperation and disbelief. Beneath his bushman's hat his face was coolly angular with a firm nose and an unyielding look to his jaw. Darcy found herself looking into a pair of wintry grey eyes and hastily revised her first impression.

He looked *very* unfriendly.

'What do you think you're doing?' he asked curtly, making no attempt to return her greeting.

Darcy looked at him in surprise, a little affronted by his tone. Men usually reacted to her smile quite differently. 'I wanted to be sure you'd see me,' she explained.

The man looked at her umbrella. It was bright yellow and green and cleverly designed as a banana tree with each spoke marking the point of a leaf and jolly bunches of bananas hanging from the middle. A friend had given it to Darcy for her birthday, and she loved it.

He didn't look as if he shared her sense of fun. 'I could hardly avoid seeing you,' he said in a deep Australian drawl that still somehow managed to sound crisp, and his gaze left the garish umbrella to travel down over Darcy's scarlet jacket and narrow striped trousers to the ridiculously unsuitable shoes that were now clogged with thick, orangey red mud. 'You don't exactly blend into the background,' he added disapprovingly. 'It's over two hundred miles to the nearest town. I want to know what you're doing wandering along here as if it were some shopping mall.'

Darcy wasn't used to being treated with such brusqueness, but since this rude man appeared to be her only chance of a lift she decided that it was best to ignore it.

'My car got stuck in the mud,' she explained.

'So that's your car I passed before the creek?'

Beneath her banana leaves, Darcy nodded. 'I'm sorry if it was in your way, but it was completely bogged. I couldn't move it forwards or backwards, so I just had to leave it.'

The rain chose that moment to redouble its efforts, crashing down on the umbrella and on the roof of the car, and effectively drowning out his reply. 'You'd better get in,' he shouted, and leant across the bench seat to open the passenger door.

Darcy slipped and slid her way round the bonnet, too relieved at the prospect of getting out of the rain to object to the unenthusiastic invitation. 'Thank you,' she gasped, manoeuvring herself into the seat and shaking out her umbrella vigorously before attempting to scrape the worst of the thick mud from her shoes. They were utterly ruined, she noticed ruefully; if she had known the outback was going to be a sea of mud, she would have brought her gumboots with her.

The roar of the rain was deadened as she pulled the door closed, marooning them in the shelter of the cab, although it still drummed on the roof in frustration and sluiced down the windscreen. Darcy shivered and stored her precious umbrella down by her feet before turning to take stock of her rescuer.

He had switched on the overhead light and was regarding her with ill-concealed impatience. There was something austere about him, Darcy decided, studying him covertly. Used to the flamboyance of the theatrical world, she was struck by his air of cool reserve, a kind of quiet, contained strength that was somehow overwhelming. It wasn't a face that gave much away. The planes of his face were lean, his features strong and sharply defined, and there was a distinctly cool set to his mouth. This wouldn't be a man who showed his emotions easily, thought Darcy, who was fond of instant analysis. Even so, it wasn't hard to tell that he was less than impressed with *her*. His mouth was turned down at the corners and the cold grey eyes were uncomfortably observant.

Under his disapproving gaze, Darcy felt herself flush, realising for the first time what an odd spectacle she must have presented, tripping along in the middle of nowhere beneath her banana umbrella. 'I'm terribly grateful,' she said, suddenly conscious too of how English she sounded, and tried her smile again.

It had no more effect than before. 'You should never leave your car in country like this,' he told her in a stringent tone. 'Why didn't you stay with your vehicle and wait for someone to come and help?'

'I thought it would be quicker to walk,' said Darcy.

'*Walk*?' echoed the man incredulously, staring at her as if she had proposed cartwheeling to the moon. 'Where to?'

'I'm on my way to a property called Bindaburra,' she said with dignity.

'You'd have been in for a long walk,' he said grimly. 'It's a good thirty kilometres to the homestead from here.'

Darcy's blue eyes widened in dismay. 'But on the map it looks as if it's just off the main track! I thought it would be just round the next bend.'

'I can only suggest that you look at the scale next time you attempt a bit of map-reading,' he said with a caustic look. 'It would make better sense than heading off into the unknown like a complete idiot.'

'How was I supposed to know it would be that far?' said Darcy a little sulkily.

'That's the whole point—you *don't* know, and in those circumstances you never leave your car, no matter how close you think you are. It's very easy to get lost out here, even when the track looks obvious, and you'd have been wandering around in the dark, which would have made it even easier. We would have found your car eventually, but we might never have found you.'

'Well, you did find me,' Darcy pointed out crossly, beginning to wish that he hadn't. A thirty-kilometre walk might have been preferable to being rescued by this disagreeably unsympathetic man. Why wasn't he rushing chivalrously to tow her car out of the mud instead of lecturing her about outback safety?

'Only by chance,' he said dampeningly. 'What do you want at Bindaburra anyway? There aren't any camping facilities there, if that's what you're hoping.'

'Camping?' Darcy stared at him in astonishment. 'Who would want to camp in *this*?' she asked, gesturing largely at the rain.

'I thought you might be looking for somewhere to spend the night instead of driving on to Muroonda,' he said. 'Obviously I was wrong.'

'I'd rather drive back to London than camp,' she assured him. She had never been near a tent in her life and she didn't intend to start now!

He looked at her with some exasperation. 'If you're not looking for somewhere to stay, what *are* you doing here?'

'What's it to do with you?' said Darcy, who was fed up with the inquisition.

'Since I own Bindaburra, I think I'm entitled to an explanation, don't you?'

Darcy stared at him. 'I think I'm the one who's entitled to an explanation,' she said in a frosty voice. 'I was under the impression that *I* owned Bindaburra!'

There was a moment's frozen silence. His hand had closed convulsively on the steering-wheel at her announcement and the black brows snapped together.

'*What* . . . ?' he began in disbelief, then stopped. To Darcy's astonishment, his angry expression changed to one of exasperated resignation. 'Don't tell me!' he said wearily. 'You're Darcy.'

'Miss Meadows to you!' Darcy's eyes flashed dangerously blue. She could hardly believe the effrontery of the man. He didn't even look embarrassed at having been caught blatantly lying! This must be some station hand who was taking advantage of Uncle Bill's death. Well, he wouldn't be taking advantage much longer; he had her to deal with now! 'How dare you tell people that you own my property?'

'Because it's not your property——' he began with infuriating calm, but Darcy interrupted him.

'It most certainly is!' She glared, digging into her bag to produce an envelope which she waved at him. 'This is a letter from solicitors in Adelaide informing me of my great-uncle's death and that I was his sole beneficiary. Read it if you don't believe me!'

'Oh, I believe you, *Miss Meadows*,' he said with an edge of contempt. 'I just wasn't expecting you to rush out quite so quickly to see what you'd got out of the old man, that's all.'

'What do you mean by that?' demanded Darcy furiously. 'Who *are* you?'

'My name's Cooper Anderson.' He watched her closely for a reaction, but by now Darcy was too angry to notice.

'Well, Mr Anderson, you can consider yourself unemployed as from now!' she said with magnificent disregard for the fact that she had been relying on him to rescue her. She would rather walk, she decided, and was reaching for the door-handle when Cooper stopped her.

'I hate to disappoint you, but you can't sack me,' he said.

'Give me one good reason why not!'

'If you'd let me finish earlier, I would have told you that Bindaburra isn't your property, it's *ours*. I'm your partner.'

Darcy looked at him, aghast. 'What are you talking about?' she said faintly. 'I haven't got a partner!'

'I'm afraid you have,' said Cooper. To Darcy's chagrin, he seemed more amused than offended by her appalled expression. The cool eyes gleamed and there was an intriguing suspicion of a smile about his mouth. 'I can assure you that I don't like the idea any more than you do.'

Darcy wrenched her mind away from the lurking humour in his face and clutched the solicitor's letter like a talisman. 'But Uncle Bill left all his property to me! The solicitors said so.'

'He did,' Cooper agreed coolly, his smile vanishing. 'But he only owned fifty per cent of Bindaburra. Unfortunately for you, I own the other half.'

The downpour had exhausted itself, and was now no more than a weary patter on the roof. Darcy looked at the rain dribbling down the windscreen and struggled to assimilate the idea of having a partner. 'I suppose you can prove this?' she said after a moment.

'I should hardly have bothered telling you if I couldn't,' he pointed out with some acidity.

Darcy bit her lip. 'I didn't realise... Uncle Bill never said anything about having a partner...'

'It might have been sensible to have found out a little more before you rushed out to claim your inheritance,' said Cooper astringently as she trailed off.

This thought had already occurred to Darcy, but it didn't make it any more welcome. She eyed her new partner with hostility. 'I wanted to come and see if everything was all right,' she said bravely. 'There might have been any number of problems on the property, with nobody to deal with them. Given that I didn't know I had a partner then, I thought the sensible decision was to come out as soon as I could.'

Cooper raised an eyebrow. Darcy didn't look like a girl much given to sensible decisions. Her eyes were a huge midnight-blue in a vivid face, and the dark, wavy hair that tumbled to her shoulders was spangled with rain. She looked vibrant, glamorous, dazzling, but definitely not sensible.

'It's a nice thought,' he said drily, reluctant amusement bracketing his mouth again. 'But you don't know anything about running a property like this. How did you propose solving any problems that you might find?'

Darcy didn't like the way that lurking smile made her heart miss a beat. 'I'm very adaptable,' she said loftily, trying to ignore it.

'Irresponsible is the word that springs to my mind,' said Cooper. Darcy thought he sounded just like her father.

'I am not irresponsible!'

'How else would you describe turning up here out of the blue?' he asked. 'Why didn't you let me know you were coming?'

'How could I do that when I didn't even know you existed?'

'You could have thought to let someone know you were coming,' he said with a gesture of impatience. 'Or did you just assume that there would be someone at the homestead, the same way you assumed that Bindaburra would be round the next bend?'

This was pretty close to the mark, but Darcy had no intention of admitting it. 'I remember Uncle Bill talking about the men who worked for him, and I thought they'd be there. Surely they won't have left already?'

'No, but it so happens that they're working at one of the out-stations this week.'

'What, all of them?'

'There are only three at this time of year, but yes, all of them.'

'But isn't there anyone at the house? A cook, a housekeeper or somebody?'

'The housekeeper left last week, and I haven't got round to replacing her yet. I wasn't planning on coming back myself, but if the rain keeps up like this all the creeks will be up, and I didn't want to be stuck on the other side.' He glanced at Darcy's mutinous face. 'If I'd decided to come back earlier, or not at all, you could have been stuck out here for a week before anyone else came along. You don't know how lucky you are.'

'How come I don't feel very lucky?' grumbled Darcy who was tired of men telling her how irresponsible she was. 'It's taken me two days to get here from Adelaide, most of it along roads that don't seem to be much more than muddy swamps. I'm cold and I'm tired and I'm wet, and I've had to trudge for miles along this rotten track and I've *ruined* these shoes,' she added, recalling another grievance. 'They were my favourites too!'

'You're pretty lucky if ruining your shoes is the worst thing you can find to complain about,' said Cooper with a complete lack of sympathy, starting the engine and swinging the ute round through the mud so suddenly that Darcy had to catch hold of the dashboard to steady herself.

'Where are you going?' she asked in some alarm.

'You don't want to sit here all night, do you? We're going to get your car. If we don't go now, the creeks will all be up and we'll both be stuck here.'

Darcy supposed she ought to be glad he wasn't intending to leave her there as he obviously wanted to, but the thought of wallowing around in the mud trying to extricate the car and then negotiate another thirty kilometres made her feel quite exhausted.

Fortunately, the creek had risen so dramatically since she had picked her way across it earlier that Cooper decided that they couldn't afford to waste time towing out the car.

'We'll just collect your things and go,' he said, peering out of his window at the water level as they bumped slowly across the creek bed.

'Does it always rise this fast?' asked Darcy nervously, taken aback by the power of the water swirling around the wheels.

'It does when it rains like this. There are another five creeks between here and Bindaburra, too, so the sooner we cross them the better.'

The car sat where she had left it, ploughed into a deep trough of mud. In spite of her relief at not having to drive any further, Darcy eyed it doubtfully. 'Do you think it will be all right just to leave it here?'

'If it carries on raining like this, no one's going to be along to steal it, if that's what you're worried about,' said Cooper, looking resigned as Darcy put up her banana umbrella fastidiously before slithering through the mud to unlock the car. 'No one would want a car like this, anyway,' he added, and gave one of the tyres a disparaging kick. 'This kind of thing is worse than useless out here. It's a miracle you didn't get bogged before this. Why didn't you hire a four-wheel drive?'

'I couldn't afford it,' she said simply, opening the boot to reveal a suitcase and a bulging stuff bag.

Cooper lifted out the suitcase. 'You seem to have been able to afford a flight to Australia at short notice,' he pointed out.

'My father lent me the money for the ticket,' Darcy confessed. 'I didn't know how long it would take to get here from Adelaide, so I had to hire a car, but I thought I should get the cheapest in case I couldn't take it back after a few days.' She hoisted out the stuff bag and banged the boot shut. 'It's just as well I did! I didn't realise it would take two days just to get here!'

'There seem to be a lot of things you didn't realise about Bindaburra,' said Cooper unpleasantly, tossing the case into the open back of the ute.

Darcy peered in after it. 'It's going to get a bit wet like that, isn't it?'

'Not as wet as we're going to be if we don't get moving,' he said, but she was reluctant to give up on her case that easily.

'Isn't there room inside?'

'Not unless you'd like to have it on your lap,' said Cooper impatiently.

'My clothes are going to be sodden,' Darcy complained. 'Couldn't we cover it with something?'

Muttering under his breath, Cooper unearthed a grubby tarpaulin from beneath the clutter of tools, jerricans and ropes and threw it over the case. 'There! Happy now?'

'I suppose so,' said Darcy, gloomily contemplating a case full of damp clothes.

'In that case, will you please shut up and get in? If the creeks keep rising, your wet clothes are going to be the least of our problems!'

In the event, they made it across all the creeks— but only just. Each one was deeper and more alarming, until the water in the last was swirling over Darcy's feet. She swallowed. The car she had hired would never have got through, and she would have been in real trouble if she had been stuck in the middle of the creek. Perhaps she ought to be a little more grateful that Cooper had come along after all.

It was completely dark by the time they arrived at Bindaburra homestead, and Darcy was too relieved at having reached it safely to be disappointed that she couldn't see more of the house. She had a confused

impression of a long, low house with a deep veranda
before Cooper led her down a dim corridor lit by a
single naked electric light bulb and opened a door.
'This is where the last housekeeper slept, so it
shouldn't be in too bad a state,' he said, dumping her
cases inside. 'I'll find you some sheets, and I presume
you'd like a shower, but then we'd better talk.'

He made it sound rather ominous. Left alone,
Darcy sat rather uncertainly on the bed and looked
around her. It was a plain room, with spartan, old-
fashioned furnishings and that indefinable smell of
emptiness. Suddenly she felt rather forlorn. She had
imagined a bright, welcoming house bathed in bright
sunshine, not rain and gloom and a hostile partner.
She should have listened to her father and stayed at
home, she thought glumly.

She felt better after a shower. Lugging her suitcase
over to the bed, she draped the damp clothes over
a chair and burrowed down to find something dry.
Eventually she pulled out a dress made of soft, fine
wool that swirled comfortingly about her. It was a
wonderfully rich colour, somewhere between deep blue
and purple, with a narrow waist emphasised by a wide
suede belt. Darcy pushed a selection of Middle Eastern
bracelets up her arm and regarded herself critically in
the mirror.

The dim light gave her the look of a Forties film
star, just catching the silky gleam of dark hair and
making her eyes seem bigger and bluer than ever. Why
was Cooper so determinedly unimpressed? True, she
didn't look like the most practical girl in the world,
but she was pretty and friendly and—whatever he
might think—not completely brainless. What was so
wrong with that?

Darcy gave herself an encouraging smile that faded as she remembered how Cooper had simply ignored it. She had never met anyone so resistant to her charms. It wasn't that she wanted him to find her attractive, she reminded herself hastily, but he could have been a little more...welcoming.

Her bracelets chinked against each other as she walked down the long, ill-lit corridor. She found Cooper in the kitchen, a large, old-fashioned room with a row of steel fridges and an antiquated-looking stove.

Cooper was sitting at the scrubbed wooden table, turning a can of beer absently between his hands. His face was intent with thought and there was a slight crease between his brows, as if he was pondering some difficult problem, but he looked up at Darcy's approach, his clear, cool grey gaze meeting her warm blue one across the room.

Darcy stopped dead in the doorway, overwhelmed by a sudden and inexplicable sense of recognition at the sight of him. The line of his cheek, the curl of his mouth, the long brown fingers against the beer can, all suddenly seemed almost painfully familiar. It was as if she had always known him, had already traced the angles of his face with her hands and counted each crease at the edges of his eyes. Darcy felt jarred, breathless, quite unprepared for the peculiar certainty that her whole life had led to this moment, standing in a strange kitchen, staring into the eyes of this cool, watchful man while a clock ticked somewhere in the silence and outside the rain drummed noisily on the corrugated-tin roof.

'What's the matter?' Cooper got to his feet, frowning.

Thoroughly unnerved by her bizarre reaction, Darcy swallowed. 'Nothing,' she croaked, and cleared her throat hastily. 'Should there be?'

'You look a bit peculiar.'

'I was under the impression that you thought that everything about me was peculiar,' she said waspishly, desperately trying to recover herself and wishing that Cooper's eyes weren't quite so acute.

'What makes you say that?' he asked politely.

Typically, Darcy couldn't then think of a single thing he had said to hold against him. 'It's just an impression you give,' she said a little sullenly. 'You make me feel as if I'm a complete idiot.'

Cooper looked amused. 'Anyone would feel a complete idiot, carrying a ridiculous umbrella like that,' he said. He raised an eyebrow at Darcy, still hesitating in the doorway. 'Are you going to stand there all night, or would you like to come in?'

That was exactly the kind of comment she had meant, Darcy thought crossly, but of course it was impossible to explain it to him. At least that odd feeling had gone. Obscurely grateful to Cooper for reminding her that he was simply a disagreeable stranger, she went over to the table and pulled out a chair. She was tired, still jet-lagged, lost and disorientated in a strange place. Nothing else could explain that brief, swamping sense of recognition when she had stood in the doorway and looked across at Cooper.

'Like a beer?' he asked.

'I'd rather have tea if you have some,' she said, proud of how cool she sounded.

'Sure.' Cooper crossed to the sink and filled the kettle, and Darcy found herself watching him as if

she had never seen him before. There was a lean
ranginess about him that hadn't been so obvious in
the ute. His body was compact and very controlled,
and his movements had a sort of quiet, deliberate
economy that was curiously reassuring.

He could hardly have been more different from
Sebastian, she thought. Sebastian was fair and flam-
boyant, Cooper dark and unhurried, and yet Darcy
had a sudden conviction that if she put them in a room
together it would be Cooper who was the focus of
attention. He wasn't nearly as handsome as Sebastian,
but there was something much more compelling about
him than mere good looks, and for the first time she
appreciated just how alone they were together. The
outside world seemed a long, long way away.

Darcy fiddled nervously with her bracelets, but the
chinking silver sounded abnormally loud and she
forced herself to link her hands together and think of
something to say instead.

Unperturbed by the silence, Cooper had propped
himself against the cupboards while he waited for the
kettle to boil, arms folded across his chest and long
legs crossed casually at the ankles.

'How did Uncle Bill die?' Darcy asked at last. 'The
solicitor just said that he died suddenly, but he seemed
so healthy when he was in England.'

'It was a freak accident,' said Cooper quietly. 'He
broke his neck when he came off his motorbike. He'd
hit an anthill and must have fallen the wrong way.'
He paused and glanced at Darcy. 'He died instantly.'

Darcy closed her eyes. Her great-uncle had been
such a strong, colourful character that it was impossible to imagine him killed by anything as small
as an anthill.

'Is that why you came?' asked Cooper abruptly. 'To find out how he died?'

'Partly.'

'And partly to see what he'd left you?'

There was an unmistakably sardonic edge to his voice and Darcy stiffened. 'Uncle Bill always wanted me to see Bindaburra,' she said defiantly.

'He wanted you to see it; he didn't want you to have it.'

'That's not what his will said,' said Darcy in a cold voice. 'I'm his great-niece and he was fond of me. Why shouldn't he leave his property to me?'

'Because he said he would leave it to me.'

'To *you*? Why you?'

The kettle shrieked and Cooper turned calmly away to make a pot of tea. 'I was his partner. He knew he could trust me to look after Bindaburra the way he had done.'

'You can't have been partners all that long,' Darcy objected. 'Uncle Bill never mentioned you when he was in England and that was only two years ago.'

'He wouldn't have done.' Cooper put the lid back on the teapot and carried it over to the table. 'Bill hated the fact that he couldn't manage financially without a partner. I think he thought that if he didn't talk about it it would mean that Bindaburra was still completely his.'

'So were you a sort of sleeping partner?' asked Darcy as he looked in one of the fridges for some milk.

'In a way. I put in the capital he needed, but we agreed that Bill would continue to run Bindaburra without any interference from me. We had a tacit understanding that I would take over when he couldn't manage any more, and that on his death the whole property would revert to me.'

He pushed the milk across the table towards Darcy, who poured some into a mug, frowning slightly. 'Does that mean you've only taken over here since he died?'

'Exactly. I haven't had time to sort out the homestead yet, but Bindaburra will be my base.'

'Doesn't that rather depend on me?' said Darcy coolly, reaching for the teapot.

Cooper looked grim. 'It does now. Bill was a man of his word, but he obviously never got round to changing his will. I can assure you, though, that he intended Bindaburra to go to someone who could continue to look after it as he would have wanted.'

'I've only got your word for that,' she pointed out.

'You needn't worry,' said Cooper contemptuously. 'I don't expect you to honour Bill's agreement. I'll give you a good price for your share.'

Darcy stirred her tea vigorously and laid down the spoon with a click. 'Suppose I don't want to sell?'

'What else can you do?' he said with an irritable look. 'You're surely not proposing to stay here yourself?'

He made it sound such a ludicrous idea that Darcy, who hadn't got as far as proposing anything other than proving to Cooper Anderson that she had no intention of meekly giving in to whatever he suggested, sat back in her chair and pushed the chinking bracelets defiantly up her arm.

'Why not?' she said.

CHAPTER TWO

'DON'T be ridiculous!' said Cooper impatiently. 'You can't stay here.'

'I don't see why not.' Darcy was looking mutinous. 'It's my house, isn't it?'

He sucked in his breath, obviously having trouble controlling his temper. 'If this is a way of trying to get me to force up my price, you can forget it, Darcy... sorry, *Miss Meadows*.'

'I'm not interested in the money,' she said with a glare at his sarcastic reminder of the way she had mistaken him for an employee. 'I'm interested in doing what Uncle Bill would have wanted, and that doesn't include handing it over to you as soon as you wave a cheque-book under my nose!'

'Are you sure you want to turn your back on that kind of money?'

'I loved Uncle Bill,' Darcy said fiercely. 'That means far more to me than anything, and if you thought I came out here just to bump up the price of some crummy little outback station you've got another think coming!'

'Is that what you think Bindaburra is? A "crummy little outback station"?'

Darcy shifted a little uncomfortably at the sting in his voice. 'I know it didn't seem like that to Uncle Bill,' she admitted sulkily. 'I only meant that the property isn't likely to be of any interest to me financially.'

'Bindaburra covers over ten thousand square kilometres,' said Cooper coldly. 'It's a very valuable property,' he went on, ignoring Darcy's dropped jaw. 'You should consider that before you claim not to have any financial interest. Personally, I think you would be mad not to accept my offer to buy your share from you. You're unlikely to be able to sell it as easily with a hostile partner already in place.'

'I had no idea it was that big,' said Darcy, struggling to convert kilometres into miles to try and work out just how big 'big' was. Not that she needed to bother. The answer was obviously *huge*.

'Perhaps now you'll realise how impossible it would be for you to stay!'

Darcy lifted her chin stubbornly. 'No.'

'Bindaburra can't support someone who just sits around looking decorative,' said Cooper with a scathing look, and she bristled.

'I don't just *sit around*! I'm used to working.'

'Oh, yes?' He didn't even bother to hide his disbelief. 'Doing what?'

'I'm an actress.'

'Oh, an *actress* ... that'll be handy!' Cooper was predictably sarcastic. 'I'm talking about real work.'

'Acting is work,' she protested. 'It's much harder work than most people realise. It only looks easy.'

'It's still not exactly relevant experience for running a cattle station, is it?'

Darcy took a defiant sip of her tea. 'I could learn.'

'We're not talking about a part in some play!' A muscle hammered in Cooper's lean jaw. 'Bill worked hard all his life to build up Bindaburra into one of the finest properties in this part of Australia. I'm not going to let you throw it all away. Quite apart from anything else, I've got my investment to consider. That's why I am now running Bindaburra, and I'm more than capable of running it without assistance from you!'

'And I've got my inheritance to consider,' she retorted. 'What about all these other properties you said you owned? How do I know that you won't be so busy that you'll end up neglecting Bindaburra?'

Cooper clenched his teeth together. 'There's no question of that. I have managers who deal with problems on a day-to-day basis, and I've already made arrangements to come and live here permanently.'

'That was a bit premature, wasn't it? You could at least have waited to see what I wanted to do!'

'It never occurred to me that you would want to do anything other than sell,' he snapped. 'I certainly didn't think you would drop everything and hotfoot it out from England to see exactly what the old man had left you!'

'It wasn't like that,' Darcy protested, stung.

'It looks like that from where I'm standing. You and your family ignored Bill for forty years. It was only when he went over to England and looked you up that you suddenly discovered that he owned a cattle station and you started making a fuss of him. Oh, there have been plenty of letters since then but it's funny how you've only kept in touch since you thought you might get something out of him—as you have.'

Darcy banged her mug down on the table so hard that tea slopped over the edge. 'I've told you, I had no idea that Bindaburra was worth anything!'

'So you say. I've only got your word for that.'

'Well, you'll just have to take it, then, won't you?'

'I will if you'll take my word that Bill intended to leave Bindaburra to me,' said Cooper in a hard voice.

There was a hostile silence as they glared stubbornly at each other. It was Darcy who spoke first. 'It sounds as if you've got other properties. Why do I have to sell up just so that you can have another one?'

He hesitated. 'Bindaburra's special,' he said after a moment. 'I've waited for this property a long time. I want all of Bindaburra, and I don't care what I have to do to get it. If that means paying you a fair and generous price for something that's rightfully mine, then that's what I'll have to do, but I'm not prepared to play silly games with you about it.'

'I've got no intention of playing games,' said Darcy, angrily shaking back her dark hair. 'What makes Bindaburra rightfully yours? If Uncle Bill had wanted you to have Bindaburra, then he would have left it to you, but he didn't. I came out here not because I wanted to see what I'd "got out of him", as you put it, but because I felt I owed it to Uncle Bill to come. If he left Bindaburra to me, it's because he wanted me to have it, not you, and I'm not going to casually hand it over on your say-so, no matter how fair and generous you think your offer is!'

Cooper crunched his empty beer can in his hand with an angry exclamation. 'Fine words, but why don't you face facts? A cattle station is no place for someone like you. It's a hard, uncomfortable life, and you wouldn't last five minutes out here on your own.'

'Perhaps, but I'm still not going to be bullied into selling,' said Darcy, draining her tea and pushing back her chair to stand up. 'You've made it very plain that you don't want me here, but you're not going to get rid of me that easily. I may well decide to sell, but I'll make up my own mind in my own time, and until I do I'm going to stay, so you'll just have to lump it, won't you?'

In spite of her brave words, Darcy lay awake wondering what on earth she had got herself into. It was wet and miserable, the house was cold and dingy and she was stuck in the middle of nowhere with a man who apparently both disliked and distrusted her. If she had any sense, she would take whatever Cooper Anderson was offering and head back for civilisation as soon as she could.

No, Darcy corrected herself gloomily. If she had any sense she wouldn't have come at all.

Cooper was right—there was nothing for her here. She was an actress—she needed lights, music, people, an audience. Cooper was very unsatisfactory. He wasn't in the least bit sympathetic, and showed no inclination to admire or applaud. Darcy longed to ring up half a dozen friends and ask their opinion; she was already getting withdrawal symptoms from not having a phone. It would be easy to describe her arrival at Bindaburra, more difficult to explain what Cooper was like.

Drawing the blankets up round her chin, Darcy rolled over on to her side and stared into the darkness. At first sight he seemed a typical outback type, with that lean, rangy body and the air of unhurried deliberation, but there was nothing typical about those penetrating eyes or that mouth . . .

Darcy clamped down firmly on thoughts of Cooper's mouth and threw herself on to her other side with much readjustment of blankets. Much better to think about how arrogant and disagreeable he was. She frowned as she remembered how contemptuous he had been about her relationship with her great-uncle. It was true that the family had ignored him for forty years, but that was because they hadn't known that he was still alive. Bill had left for Australia in 1924 after a bitter row with Darcy's grandfather, and nothing had been heard from him since their mother had died just after the war. Until two years ago, that was, when Bill had turned up at the house that Darcy's parents still lived in. They had been surprised, but delighted to welcome him back into the family. When Darcy had met him, she had been amazed that this stocky, pugnaciously colourful Australian could possibly be related to her grandfather, whom she dimly remembered as a stiff and punctiliously correct figure.

Both her parents had been occupied with other things that summer, so it had been Darcy who had spent the most time with her great-uncle. They could hardly have been more different, but each had struck a chord in the other, and much to everyone's surprise, not least their own, they had enjoyed each other's company. Darcy had swept her great-uncle off to parties and introduced him to all her friends with a complete lack of inhibition, and Bill had been in turns alarmed, astounded, suspicious and finally charmed.

Remembering her uncle made Darcy glad she had come. He had always wanted her to see Bindaburra, and see it she would, Cooper Anderson or no Cooper Anderson! She knew perfectly well that she wasn't capable of running the property by herself, but she was damned if she was tamely going to hand everything over to Cooper. She would have to sell in the end, she supposed, but in the meantime she had a perfect right to be here, and it wouldn't do him any harm to sweat a little!

It was still raining the next morning. Darcy had finally fallen into a deep, exhausted sleep which left her feeling jaded and disorientated and she rubbed her eyes with the heel of her hand as she wandered down the corridor to the kitchen, pulling her dressing-gown about her. It was an old one of her father's, a dark red Paisley-pattern silk that had become a little worn over the years but which was still Darcy's favourite. She hadn't thought to bring any slippers, though, and her feet were cold on the polished wooden floor.

It was so dark that Cooper had the light on in the kitchen. He was standing looking out at the rain as he drank a mug of tea, but he turned as Darcy came yawning into the kitchen. She was never at her best in the morning. Her blue eyes were still smudgy with sleep and the thick dark hair tumbled wildly about her face.

An unreadable expression flickered over Cooper's face as he watched her pad over to the kettle, but his voice was as astringent as Darcy remembered. 'You'll have to get up earlier than this if you're planning to run the property,' he said, looking pointedly at his watch.

'It's only half-past nine,' said Darcy, squinting at her own watch.

'It's quarter to ten.'

'Oh, well, that's more or less half-past nine.' Oblivious to Cooper's stare, she peered into a cupboard. 'Is there any fresh coffee?'

'I doubt it very much,' said Cooper. 'Bill lived a very frugal existence. If you're looking for luxuries, you've come to the wrong place. You'll find some instant in the cupboard below,' he added. 'Do you want some breakfast?'

Darcy shook her dark head. 'I can only cope with coffee at this time of the morning,' she confessed. 'You go ahead and have some, though.'

Looking up from stirring her coffee, she caught the gleam of amusement in his grey eyes. 'I've already had breakfast, thank you,' he said. 'Four hours ago. I've just come in for a cup of tea.'

With some difficulty, Darcy mentally subtracted four hours. 'You had breakfast at five-thirty?' she asked incredulously.

'You'd better get used to it if you're still planning to stay. Or has a good night's sleep made you see things in a more sensible light?'

'I haven't changed my mind, if that's what you mean,' said Darcy, although privately she doubted that she would be able to bear any regime which meant getting up at five o'clock, and as for eating breakfast then . . . ! She shuddered at the thought.

Shifting from foot to foot on the cold floor, she made herself a coffee and went to sit cross-legged on a chair, tucking her feet up beneath her. 'It's freezing,' she grumbled and cradled her hands around the mug. 'I thought this was supposed to be a desert?'

'It is mid-winter,' Cooper pointed out. 'You should be glad it's like this.'

'How do you work that one out?' she asked, still grumpy with sleep.

'If you're going to be part-owner of a property like Bindaburra, you're going to have to learn to pray for rain. If we don't have rain, we don't have feed for the cattle, and if we can't feed our stock we'll *both* be selling up.'

Darcy stared morosely at the rain pouring off the roof of the veranda outside the kitchen window. Surely they had had enough rain in the last two days to be going on with? It was June, summer at home. Everyone would sitting outside the pubs in the sunshine, walking across the parks in bare feet, drinking Pimms in the garden. Of course, it might be raining at home, too, she admitted honestly.

Cooper came over to the table and pulled out a chair. Darcy watched him a little warily. He looked bigger in daylight, and everything about him was more pronounced. She was very conscious suddenly of his solidity and the latent power of his body, and she thought of the French expression—being at ease in one's skin. It described Cooper perfectly. He was quiet and controlled and somehow centred.

He must have been outside for his face had a damp sheen and his eyelashes were still wet. Darcy found herself staring at them. They were short and thick and the rain had emphasised how their darkness contrasted with the startling lightness of his eyes. For no reason, a tiny shiver slid down her spine and she pulled her dressing-gown closer around her.

'How long had you intended to stay?' he asked abruptly.

'As long as necessary,' said Darcy, irritated by that 'had'. She put up her chin. 'I booked a return flight to London in a month's time, but I can easily change it if I decide to stay longer.'

'I wouldn't have thought a busy actress could afford to be away that long.'

'It just so happens that I don't have any commitments at the moment,' said Darcy in a dignified way. She was rather sensitive about the fact that the play that had given her her first big break had turned out to be a flop, and had folded after a disastrous two weeks.

'Ah,' said Cooper with one of his disquieting gleams of humour. 'So you're...what's the word...*resting*?'

She gave him a cold look. 'That's one way of putting it, yes.'

'What happens if a starring role comes up while you're away?'

That was about as likely as one of his cows jumping over the moon, but Darcy didn't feel like telling Cooper that. She had spent the last six weeks sitting by the phone, but no call to instant stardom had come, and, while she was normally the most optimistic of souls, she couldn't help thinking that a month or two away wouldn't mean missing more than a couple of television adverts. Still, it wouldn't do for Cooper to guess that she was something less than a household name.

'Naturally, I'll have to let my agent know how she can contact me,' she said grandly.

'I hope she knows how to use a radio,' said Cooper in a dry voice. 'Bill didn't have a phone, but if it's an emergency she can always leave a message with the Flying Doctor Service.'

Darcy tried to imagine her perennially harassed agent coping with the Flying Doctor Service. 'I'll send her the details,' she said, avoiding the sceptical glint in Cooper's eye. 'There's nothing to stop me staying here as long as I want.'

'So you won't reconsider your decision not to sell?'

'I didn't decide not to sell,' said Darcy. 'I decided not to make a decision yet, and I have no intention of changing my mind about *that*!'

To her surprise, Cooper looked resigned rather than angry. 'I didn't think you would,' he said. 'You may not have had much in common with Bill, but you seem to be just as stubborn as he was. It seems to me that the sooner I accept that the better.'

Darcy eyed him suspiciously. Cooper Anderson hadn't seemed to her the sort of man who gave in that easily. 'What are you suggesting?'

'A truce,' he said. 'I've just been out to check the creeks, and they're way up. Whatever you decide to do, we're stuck here for the next few days at least, so we may as well make the best of it. I think that means facing facts.'

'What sort of facts?' she asked cautiously.

'The fact that we're not going to agree about what Bill wanted for Bindaburra, for instance. I think—I know—that he wanted me to have it and you think he intended to leave it to you. It's obvious that neither of us is going to change our mind.' He paused and looked thoughtfully across at Darcy. 'We got off to a bad start last night. You were tired, and I wasn't expecting to have a partner thrust into my plans. Let's say that neither of us was at our best. You didn't like me and I didn't like you, and we both think the other is being unreasonable.'

He quirked an eyebrow at her, obviously waiting for her to agree. Trying to ignore an unpleasant sinking feeling at the cool way he had admitted that he didn't like her, Darcy nodded. She didn't like not being liked, and she wasn't used to such brutal candour.

'I suggest that we start again,' Cooper went on. 'You've said you've booked a flight for a month's time, and I can't make you leave before then. Since for reasons best known to yourself you seem determined to stay, I think we should try and forget about what Bill wanted and assume that we're willing partners. It'll mean that we both have to make an effort, but we ought to be able to manage that if it's just for a month.'

'Why just a month?' said Darcy.

He met her gaze directly. 'I think a month will be quite long enough to persuade you that you'd be better off selling your share to me.'

'And if it doesn't?'

'Then we can talk again.' He pushed his mug away from him. 'If you agree to this, though, it's on the understanding that we'll treat each other as partners. That means that you do your fair share of the work. You won't be a guest, and I won't treat you as one— unless, of course, you decide to sell. If you stay, you work, and if you still want to stay after a month... well, I'll admit that I was wrong.'

Darcy swirled her coffee in her mug and considered the proposal. She had a nasty feeling it wasn't going to work to her advantage, but it was hard to find anything to object to. She could hardly refuse his overture of peace, nor would she be in a very strong position if she said she didn't want to work. Perhaps she had been a little quick to imply that she wanted to run Bindaburra herself, and she suspected that Cooper was going to call her bluff by setting her impossible tasks.

'Will I have to brand cows and wrestle bulls to the ground?' she asked nervously.

Cooper looked as if he didn't know whether to be exasperated or amused. 'You're welcome to try, but that wasn't quite what I had in mind.'

'What *did* you have in mind?' said Darcy, trying to conceal her relief.

'Bill always had a housekeeper who cooked for him and the men and kept this place in some sort of order. The last girl left a couple of weeks ago, and I haven't had time to do anything about finding a replacement yet. One of the men has been doing the cooking since then, but he's more useful to me outside, so if you took over the cooking you'd be making more than a token contribution.'

Darcy toyed with the idea of objecting to the sexist way he had assumed that all she was good for was cooking and cleaning, but when she thought that the alternative might be fencing in the rain or much worse she decided that she might be better off in the kitchen after all.

'I'm not a very good cook,' she warned him, with judicious understatement. Her dinner parties made popular disaster stories among her friends and she had learnt that it was easier to buy prepared meals from the supermarket freezers to shove in the microwave.

'You must be better than Darren,' said Cooper. 'They don't want anything fancy, just roasts and stews, and a cake or a biscuit for smoko.'

'Oh, well, I expect I could manage that,' said Darcy optimistically. The more she thought about it, the more she liked the idea of working, even if it did have to be in the unglamorous role of housekeeper. Uncle Bill would have wanted her to stay, at least for a while, she told herself. If she could prove her worth to Cooper, it would be a way of showing that her great-uncle had not been mistaken in her. She would be doing it for him as much as for herself.

Fired with enthusiasm, she beamed across the table at Cooper. Her hair was still tousled from sleep, but the dark blue eyes were wide awake now. 'All right, I'll do it.'

If she had expected Cooper to look delighted, she was disappointed. Instead he sounded almost disapproving of her ready acceptance of his idea. 'There are other things you should think about as well,' he said.

'Like what?'

'Can you afford to stay, for a start? Obviously it won't cost you anything to stay here, but you won't earn anything either. It would be a pity if you gave up opportunities at home just to prove a point out here.'

'I don't see that that's a problem,' said Darcy. 'It's not as if I had any responsibilities. I share a flat with a friend. We only pay a nominal rent because her father owns it, so I won't be leaving her in the lurch. And as for work...well, as I said, I'll let my agent know how to contact me just in case something unexpected comes up.'

'Hmm.' Cooper studied her critically, unimpressed by her insouciant attitude. 'You should also consider how you feel about living alone with me.'

Carried away by the prospect of proving that she wasn't as useless as he thought her, Darcy had forgotten how she had sat fidgeting with her bracelets, overwhelmed by that strange sense of awareness. Now she uncrossed her legs and dropped her feet to the floor, conscious for the first time of the intimacy of the situation. She hadn't thought twice before about the propriety of sitting opposite him with nothing on under her dressing-gown, but now she tightened the belt automatically. The silk slithered sleekly against her skin and she had a sudden disturbing awareness of her own body.

She wished Cooper had never mentioned the prospect of living alone. She had been happily defiant before; now she couldn't take her eyes off his hands, horrified by how easily she could imagine what it would be like to sit here like lovers, still sleepy and smiling after a night together, her body tingling with remembered desire. So vivid was the picture that Darcy's skin seemed to burn as if she could feel his hands easing the dressing-gown apart to slide caressingly over her body and pull her against his tautly muscled strength . . .

Darcy swallowed and pushed the vision aside with an effort. Living alone with Cooper suddenly seemed fraught with unsuspected dangers, none of which she could explain. 'W-we won't be alone, though, will we?' she said in a voice that sounded ridiculously high even to her own ears. 'The other men will be back as soon as the creeks go down, won't they?' There would be safety in numbers, she reasoned, and with three other men around there would be none of the intimacy that might lead to more dangerous fantasising about just one.

'They'll eat with us here in the homestead, but they sleep in their own quarters.'

'Oh.' Darcy looked down into her empty coffee-mug. 'Well, couldn't you sleep in their quarters?'

'I could, but I have no intention of doing so,' said Cooper in an acerbic tone. He got up impatiently and carried his mug over to the sink. 'I intend to make

Bindaburra my home, and I don't see why I should move out just to make you feel better.'

'You were the one who brought up the subject,' she pointed out with a touch of sullenness.

'I'm just advising you to think about what's involved,' he said austerely, swirling the mug under the tap. 'There's no point in you agreeing to stay and then suddenly getting maidenly scruples.'

'I haven't got maidenly scruples!' Darcy protested.

'Oh? Then why did you suggest I move out to the ringers' quarters?'

'I just thought it would be . . . less awkward.'

Cooper came back to the table. 'Awkward for whom?'

'Well, not exactly *awkward*——' she began, wishing she'd never opened her mouth, but he interrupted her.

'You mean you don't trust me to keep my hands off you?'

'No!' Seeing Cooper raise his eyebrows, she hurried to correct herself. 'I mean, no, I didn't mean that. That you wouldn't be able to keep your hands off me, I mean . . .' Utterly confused about what she meant by now, Darcy floundered to a halt.

'Could it be that you don't trust yourself to keep your hands off *me*, then?' he suggested provocatively.

'Certainly not!' Without thinking, she jumped to her feet, clutching her dressing-gown about her, dark hair bouncing around her face and blue eyes stormy and magnificent. 'I'm hardly likely to have any interest in *you*!'

'Why not?' Cooper came round the table towards her, but Darcy was too angry to care.

'Why? *Why?*' she echoed, trying desperately to think of a convincing reason. 'Because . . . because you're just not my type, and even if you were I . . . I'm already involved with someone else,' she finished in a rush.

It didn't seem to have much effect in halting Cooper's advance, which she had belatedly noticed. 'What's his name?' he asked, calmly taking her waist between his hands. They were hard and strong and seemed to burn through the silk on to her skin.

'S-Sebastian,' she stammered, trying to push away his steely grip.

'Sebastian? Is he an actor, too?'

'Yes,' said Darcy, preoccupied with her futile struggle to free herself.

Cooper himself hardly seemed to notice her efforts. 'How involved is "involved"?' he said.

'I'm in love with him,' she said defiantly. She *was*, she reminded herself, remembering how heartbroken she had been.

'And is Sebastian in love with you?'

Darcy hesitated. 'Yes.' Much the safest answer, even if the least truthful. She had given up her attempts to wriggle free and had brought her hands up to his chest to ward him off. Beneath her palms she could feel the disturbingly warm solidity of his body through the brushed-cotton shirt, and she drew her hands away slightly.

'You don't sound very sure,' said Cooper conversationally, a smile lurking around his mouth.

Darcy drew a steadying breath. 'I am sure,' she said. 'Sebastian trusts me utterly.'

'Really?' he said, drawing her inexorably closer until her hands were jammed back against his chest. His eyes were alight with an expression that set her heart thudding in a treacherous combination of alarm and anticipation. 'Sebastian sounds like a rash man to me. If I were in his position, I wouldn't tempt fate by letting a girl like you out of my sight, let alone disappear off to Australia on her own.'

'He knows I'd never be interested in another man,' whispered Darcy, who could hardly hear her own voice above the booming of her heart and was fighting a desperate battle against the terrible temptation to lean into him.

Cooper's smile was speculative. 'Well, let's see if Sebastian was right or not, shall we?' he murmured, and slid his hands up to cup her throat and lift her face to his.

CHAPTER THREE

THE touch of Cooper's mouth sent a lightning bolt of reaction through her, catching Darcy off balance. It was as if the floor had dropped away beneath her, plunging her into a maelstrom of conflicting emotions, and she gasped, clutching instinctively at the front of his shirt as her only anchor.

How had she known that his lips would be so warm, so sure, so treacherously persuasive? Darcy was caught between shock and the arrowing certainty that it had always been like this. Just as when she had hesitated in the kitchen door last night she had been swamped by that strange sense of familiarity, so now his kiss left her awash with recognition. It was almost like coming home; the touch and the scent and the hard, masculine feel of his body through the flimsy silk dressing-gown were all part of her, inseparable from the intoxicating rush of feeling that swirled through her senses and left her reeling and incapable of thought.

She was unaware of her hands slowly loosening their clutch on his shirt to spread and slide over his chest and up to his shoulders. Beneath the cotton, his body was tempered steel, solid and unyielding to her touch. Darcy clung to its reassuring strength, heedless of the instinctive arch of her body. Her head was tipped back invitingly so that her soft dark hair fell over his hand, which was smoothing seductively down her spine. She had forgotten her anger, forgotten Sebastian and the cold floor beneath her bare feet, forgotten everything but Cooper's kiss, his mouth on hers, his hands burning through the silk on to her skin and the breathtaking thump of excitement that was beating ever louder and faster, drowning out the voice that should have been shouting at her to resist.

As her arms slid round his neck, Cooper lifted his mouth from hers, but only to gather her closer again into a kiss that was deeper and more demanding than before. Darcy was drowning, dissolving in a rising tide of desire, and her fingers tightened on his shoulders as the silk belt of her gown slithered apart and his hands slipped beneath to curve over her body. Darcy gasped aloud, electrified by their scorching exploration, and sheer, shameful pleasure shuddered over her skin.

Abandoned to the wash of sensation, Darcy hardly heard Cooper's muttered exclamation or realised that his hands had stilled abruptly. They withdrew slowly, sliding reluctantly out from beneath the silk as he levered himself away from her. By the time Darcy had grasped what was happening, he was retying her belt with a wry smile.

'I think Sebastian might have made a big mistake,' he said. 'A very big one.'

He might as well have dashed a bucket of cold water in her face. Darcy recoiled from the sharp slap of reality, aghast at her own response. White-faced, she pushed his hands away from her waist and retied the belt herself, pulling the sides of the dressing-gown together high around her throat with shaking fingers.

'That wasn't fair,' she said unsteadily.

'It wasn't particularly fair of you to sit there with nothing on under that dressing-gown either.' Quite unconcerned, Cooper propped himself against the table and calmly watched Darcy's fumbling attempts to straighten herself.

It was impossible to believe that this cool, self-contained man eyeing her with faint amusement could be the same man who had been kissing her only moments ago, the same man who had buried his face in her hair, whose hands had explored the smooth softness of her body with such devastating skill. Darcy clutched her robe about her, her eyes huge and dark. She felt disorientated and lost, almost bereft. How could he look so indifferent? Hadn't he felt *anything*?

She pulled herself together with an immense effort. If Cooper could appear so unmoved, she wasn't going to let him know just how shattered she felt. 'I know what you're doing,' she said, somehow managing to keep her voice steady. 'You just want to make me leave and you're prepared to do anything to make sure I go as soon as possible.'

'If that were what I was trying to do, I would hardly have offered you a month's truce,' Cooper pointed out coolly. 'However, now you mention it, it doesn't sound like a bad policy. *Have* I persuaded you that you'd be better off leaving as soon as the creeks are down?'

'No, you haven't!' said Darcy, who was regaining her temper with her composure. 'If you think a paltry little kiss like that is enough to scare me into leaving, you've got another think coming!'

'Does that mean you want to go ahead with a month's trial partnership?'

Darcy felt as if she had been outmanoeuvred somewhere along the line. She wanted nothing better than to tell Cooper what he could do with his trial partnership, but then she would have little option but to leave, and she wasn't going to give in that easily. 'As long as there are no more... incidents... like the one that's just taken place,' she said.

'But I thought paltry little kisses didn't bother you?'

'They don't,' said Darcy bravely and quite untruthfully. 'That doesn't mean I like them.'

'That's funny,' said Cooper. 'I was under the impression that you quite enjoyed it. I know I did.'

Darcy eyed him with acute resentment. 'I'd rather it didn't happen again,' she said in a frosty voice.

'I'll tell you what,' he said amenably. 'I won't kiss you again if you don't provoke me again.'

'I didn't provoke you!' she protested indignantly.

Cooper raised an eyebrow. 'Didn't you? It felt that way to me.'

'I can't help the way you feel,' said Darcy, ruffled as much by Cooper's calm discussion of the kiss as by the kiss itself.

'No,' he agreed, straightening from the table. To her fury, his eyes held not embarrassment but an unmistakable glint of amusement. 'You could try wearing more clothes in future, though. Now,' he went on in a brisk tone before Darcy had time to think of a suitably dignified retort, 'I suggest we abide by the terms of our truce and start work. Since there's just the two of us here, this seems like a good opportunity to clear out Bill's office. You could give me a hand— once you've changed, of course.'

Darcy made sure she covered herself from neck to toe. Her bones were still weak with remembered desire as she stood under the shower and she felt hollow whenever she thought about Cooper's mouth and Cooper's hands and the lean, hard strength of his

body. She closed her eyes, wishing she could banish
the memory of his touch, but he might as well have
been standing there still, his fingers tracing irresistible
patterns of desire on her skin, for all that she could
forget.

She felt better after pulling on jeans and a bulky
cardigan over a cotton polo-necked jumper. There,
Cooper could hardly accuse her of being dressed re-
vealingly now! Darcy had given herself a stern talking-
to, but she was more nervous than she cared to admit
about the coming month. If only she and Sebastian
really were still in love, it would make it so much
easier. She wouldn't have responded to Cooper's kiss
like that for a start, Darcy told herself, choosing to
ignore a little voice which told her that Sebastian's
kisses had never been like that. Well, she would just
have to pretend that she still was, she decided; she
wasn't an actress for nothing, and she was determined
that Cooper wasn't going to get the better of her.
Darcy had always had a stubborn streak along with
a certain instinctive contrariness when faced with a
will as strong as her own. She would stick out this
month, just to show Cooper Anderson that she could,
and what was more she would be so useful that in the
end he would beg her to stay, and she would have
great satisfaction in refusing!

It was a comforting thought, and Darcy enjoyed
herself imagining exactly what she would say to
Cooper, and how he would grovel to try and persuade
her not to go, but when she had finished dressing and
had to face him again suddenly the scene didn't seem
quite so likely. She had to muster all her acting skills
to appear cool and poised as she made her way down
the gloomy corridor to her great-uncle's old office, a

dark, poky little room at the back of the house, over-flowing with piles of letters, accounts, catalogues and old farming magazines.

Cooper was sitting at the desk, trying to clear a space among the clutter. 'What a horrible little room,' said Darcy, wrinkling her nose. 'How could Uncle Bill bear to sit in here?'

'I don't think he could,' said Cooper drily. 'He just used to throw all his papers in here and shut the door—hence the mess. No one knew the land better than Bill, but he wasn't a businessman.'

'And you are, I suppose?' Darcy was unable to prevent herself saying snidely.

He gave her a cool look. 'I own five properties in this part of South Australia, as well as several busi-nesses in Adelaide—I have to be.'

'If you're such a good businessman, why do you want Bindaburra so badly?' she asked, wrapping her cardigan more firmly about her as she wandered over to the tiny window. It was much easier to pretend to be cool and poised when she wasn't looking at him, she discovered. Bulky layers didn't seem to make much difference; under that cool, amused gaze, she might as well still be wearing the silken robe.

Cooper didn't answer immediately. 'Bindaburra is part of my family,' he said at last. 'My great-grandfather built this house in 1875, and my father was born here.'

'But not you?' Darcy turned from the window curiously.

'No.' He straightened a pile of papers on the desk in front of him. 'My grandfather lost everything in a terrible drought, and he had to sell up. That's when Bill bought the property, but my father was always bitter that he didn't inherit the place where he'd grown up, and that he couldn't pass it on to me. There's a lot of Anderson history here at Bindaburra,' he went on slowly. 'When he was dying, I promised him that if I ever got the chance I'd get Bindaburra back for my own sons.'

Darcy's heart felt as if something had slammed into it. 'I didn't know you had any children,' she said, unnerved by how clearly she could imagine them— little boys with quiet faces and observant grey eyes.

'I don't,' said Cooper. 'Or not yet, anyway. I was talking theoretically. But if I ever did have children, I'd like them to grow up here at Bindaburra.'

'Oh,' said Darcy, wishing she hadn't asked. She wondered what Cooper would be like as a father, what sort of woman he would choose to be the mother of his children. It wouldn't be anyone like her, that was for sure, she thought with an odd sinking sensation. It was all he could do to contemplate spending a month with her, let alone a lifetime. Not that she cared *whom* he married, she reassured herself hastily, and decided to change the subject.

'What shall I do?' she said, determinedly businesslike.

Cooper got up from behind the desk. 'I think it might be an idea to move the office to another room. This is far too small, and it would be easier to sort things out as we transfer them.' He led Darcy down the corridor to an unused square room looking out on to the veranda which ran down the side of the house. It was empty apart from an old wardrobe and a chest of drawers.

'It's a bit dark, isn't it?' said Darcy doubtfully. 'Couldn't we find a brighter room?'

'When it's fifty degrees outside, the last thing you want is a bright room,' Cooper pointed out. 'The whole point is to keep the house as cool and shaded as possible.'

Darcy grimaced. 'I still think it's a gloomy place to sit and work.'

'As you're highly unlikely ever to use it, I hardly think it matters,' he said caustically, and she immediately stuck out her chin.

'I might do,' she said with a challenging look.

Cooper sighed. 'Oh, all right, if you say so. It doesn't change the fact that the house is built to keep out the sun, not let it in, so this is as bright as you're going to get.'

'It doesn't look as if it's been cleaned for years,' said Darcy, running a finger along the top of the chest and grimacing at the dust.

'Bill never used this side of the house.' Cooper looked around the room. 'These would all have been bedrooms originally, but he had no use for them, so he used to keep them locked.'

No wonder the house seemed empty and forlorn. It was solidly built and, now that Darcy looked again, well-proportioned, but everything was in sore need of a good scrub and a new coat of paint. It needed more than that, she thought, unconscious of her wistful expression. It needed to be lived in. It needed a family, children to fill these sad, empty rooms, children who would look like Cooper and his sensible, practical, unknown wife.

Darcy shook herself mentally. This wasn't getting her anywhere. She was supposed to be showing Cooper how hard she could work, not wondering about a family he didn't even have yet.

'Why don't I give this room a good clean while you start sorting out the paperwork?' she suggested, and was rewarded with a look that was almost approval.

Darcy hated herself for glowing at the memory, and she threw herself into the cleaning in the hope that she could work it out of her system. Really, one minute she was furious with the man for grabbing her and kissing her like that—and she *hadn't* enjoyed it, not really—and the next she was thrilling like a schoolgirl because he had intimated that she had had a good idea! Jet-lag had done something very strange to her mental processes, she decided, sweeping the floor vigorously.

Not by nature half-hearted about anything, Darcy was determined to clean the new office until it was spotless. She took down the old blind, which was so dusty and grimy that she consigned it immediately to the dustbin, and washed down all the paintwork before cleaning the window, polishing the chest and wardrobe and finally getting down on her hands and knees to scrub the wooden floor.

Rather to her own surprise, Darcy found that she was enjoying herself. There was something satisfying about getting rid of the years of dust and cobwebs, and she sang what she could remember of her role in a musical where she had once been a lowly member of the chorus. It wasn't surprising it had been a flop, she decided ruefully as she petered out, and tried instead more memorable numbers from successful shows she *hadn't* appeared in.

Darcy was enjoying herself so much that she lost track of the time. Oblivious to her voice ringing gaily along the corridor, she sang as she scrubbed and polished, and when she had finished she celebrated by improvising a tap dance routine across the newly washed floor with the broom as an unresponsive partner. It wasn't as wooden as some actors she had worked with, she thought with a grin, and she was still smiling as she whirled around—and stopped dead as she saw Cooper standing in the doorway, watching her with amused resignation.

He clapped. Only Cooper could manage to clap sarcastically, thought Darcy, conscious suddenly of her dirty and dishevelled appearance. She had discarded her bulky cardigan and pushed up the sleeves of her white polo neck, which was looking distinctly grubby by now. She was flushed and breathless after her energetic twirl round the floor, and there was a grimy smear across her cheek where she had wiped it with the back of her hand.

'I didn't see you there,' she said, propping the broom self-consciously against the chest.

'I was enjoying the show,' said Cooper. His eyes were creased with amusement, and there was a smile lurking around his mouth. It wasn't even a real smile, thought Darcy crossly. Why did it always make her heart turn over like that? He was nodding at the broom. 'You could do with a better partner, though.'

'Sometimes you have to make the best of what you've got when it comes to partners, don't you?'

'Quite,' he said drily. He glanced around the room. 'You've done a good job in here.'

Darcy refused to allow herself to be glad that he had noticed. 'There's no need to sound so surprised!' she grumbled. 'I told you I could work.'

'Let's say I didn't think you would have any practical experience.'

'Well, there's where you're wrong,' she said, tossing back her hair so that it bounced and swung around her face. 'When you're an actor, you have to be prepared to put yourself into any situation. I once did a commercial where I was the downtrodden mum scrubbing the kitchen floor on her hands and knees while her smug friend whizzed around with a mop in half the time. You wouldn't believe how long it took to get it right! I never thought the experience would come in handy, but at least I learnt the most comfortable way to kneel!'

'I hope you've had a role as a good cook,' said Cooper, amused.

'I'm afraid not,' Darcy admitted. 'I don't usually get cast as the homely type.'

'I wonder why that could be?' he murmured. His eyes gleamed as he looked Darcy up and down. Even dusty and begrimed, there was an indefinable glamour about her. 'Not that I would have said you were a natural for the role of the downtrodden mum with a dirty kitchen floor, either.'

'Funny, that's just what the director said too,' said Darcy glumly.

Cooper laughed at that. 'Never mind, you've been very convincing cleaning this floor, anyway,' he consoled her. 'You've certainly earned your lunch. Come along, I've made some sandwiches.'

Darcy hadn't seen him laugh before and she was taken aback by the transformation as the cool, watchful face creased into humour. His teeth were very white and strong against his tan, his laugh so deep and rich that she could feel it vibrating down to her toes.

Her gaze focused suddenly on his face. He was looking at her, one eyebrow raised enquiringly, obviously waiting for her to say something, and for one terrible moment she couldn't think what he had been talking about. Then she remembered: sandwiches. How could he kiss her like that and laugh like that and then expect her to eat *sandwiches*?

'I thought I was supposed to be the cook,' she said a little breathlessly.

'You can start tonight,' said Cooper. 'I didn't want to interrupt you in the middle of your performance.'

They ate the sandwiches in Bill's old office, where Cooper had managed to clear some space on the desk. After washing her face and hands and telling herself not to be so silly—it was only a smile, for heaven's sake!—Darcy discovered that being kissed had done wonders for her appetite. The beef sandwiches tasted like the best thing she had ever had as she sat perched on her great-uncle's cracked leather chair and pushed her hair behind her ears.

'How do you start trying to clear up a muddle like this?' she asked rather indistinctly through her sandwich, glancing around the cluttered room. Fortunately Cooper had stopped smiling, but there was still something distracting about the way he sat there and ate his sandwich and it was easier to look at the mess than to look at him and remember that kiss.

'I've been having a go at the desk. Once that's clear, we can move it into the new office, which will give us somewhere to put papers from here once they're organised.' He reached for his coffee. 'I found a lot of Bill's personal stuff,' he went on, indicating a box

balanced on the edge of the desk. 'You might want
to look through it.'

Darcy brushed the crumbs off her fingers and drew
the box towards her. 'What sort of stuff is it?'

'Letters, certificates, old photographs, that kind of
thing. I didn't look at it closely, but I did find this.'
He tossed a photograph across the desk towards her
and Darcy picked it up curiously. She recognised it
as soon as she saw it.

'I remember when this was taken,' she said in delight. The photograph showed her with her great-uncle
in the garden at home. She was wearing a straw hat
and smiling with unshadowed happiness at the camera,
with Bill more bashful by her side. 'Dear Uncle Bill!'
she went on, looking down affectionately at the photo.
'He hated having his photograph taken, but he looked
just like that, didn't he?'

Cooper nodded. 'He always looked the same. It's
you that's changed.'

'Me?' Darcy held the picture away from her and
squinted at it from various angles. 'Do you think so?'
she said, surprised. 'I think I look just the same.
Maybe it's the hat? Or maybe I'm just two years
older?'

He held out his hand and she gave the photograph
back to him so that he could study it. 'It's more than
that,' he decided at last, looking up with those un-
nervingly acute eyes. 'You look like a girl here,' he
said, tapping the picture. 'Now you look like a
woman.'

Darcy could feel the colour creeping up her throat
as she slid her gaze away from his. Just when she had
managed to forget that kiss for a few moments, he
had to go and remind her of it! She knew he was

thinking of it as well; the memory shimmered in the air between them and beneath her clothes a shiver of awareness ran over her skin.

'I—I wonder what else is in here?' she said in a tight, high voice, and bent her head over the box, praying for the revealing flush to fade from her cheeks.

Her fingers fumbled as she lifted out a pile of letters. She recognised her own handwriting on several much handled envelopes, and she was glad to think that her letters had given him so much pleasure. He wasn't a writing man, he had told her, and he had never replied, but Darcy had written anyway, long, gossipy letters about the people he had met during his visit.

There were more photographs among the letters, some that people had given him on his trip to England, others brown and creased with age. Darcy recognised a sepia print of the house which had always been her home, and which had been Bill's home too before the quarrel which had sent him off to seek his fortune in Australia. She picked it up, feeling a wash of nostalgia for the graceful old house set among the gently rolling green hills. If she could be homesick after three days, what had it been like for Uncle Bill, who had been away for over fifty years? He must surely have longed sometimes for the soft lushness of England.

Beneath the letters was an old shoebox. 'What's this?' Darcy asked Cooper, lifting it out.

He shrugged. 'I didn't look. Since he left everything to you, I thought you should be the one to go through his things.'

Darcy took off the lid. There were more letters inside, very old and faded, and a photograph of a young woman with the solemn, wide-eyed look typical of old studio portraits. Judging by her dress, Darcy thought it must have been taken in the early Thirties, but what struck her most was the fact that the picture had been torn into four pieces before being painstakingly taped together again.

'Look at this.' She showed Cooper the photograph, her awkwardness forgotten. 'I wonder who she was?'

He turned the picture over. 'Violet,' he read. 'It doesn't say Violet who.'

'I think she must have been Uncle Bill's lost love,' said Darcy excitedly. She had been glancing through the letters. 'These are all from her—poor Uncle Bill obviously couldn't bear to throw them away.'

'Bill couldn't bear to throw *anything* away,' said Cooper dampeningly. 'You only have to look around you to see that.'

Darcy didn't pay any attention. She had discovered a little jeweller's box beneath all the letters, and she caught her breath as she pulled out a ring, dull and tarnished with age, but still beautiful. It was hard to imagine Uncle Bill choosing anything so delicate. It was very simple, a single pearl set between two square diamonds. Misty-eyed, Darcy slipped it on to her finger.

'Isn't it lovely?'

Cooper's sardonic look made it clear that he didn't share her enthusiasm, but Darcy was undeterred.

'It's obvious what happened,' she told him, waving her hand around so that the diamonds glimmered dully in the electric light. 'Uncle Bill and this Violet were in love, and he asked her to marry him. She must have said yes, because he went off and bought the ring, but for some reason she called it all off. Maybe her parents didn't approve ... or she was being forced to marry someone else, perhaps?' Darcy's imagination, ever fertile, was working overtime. 'Or—I know!—maybe she was desperately ill and gave Uncle Bill his ring back on her deathbed, making him promise to marry someone else, but he never would, because he knew he could never love another.'

'Yes, and maybe she just changed her mind,' said Cooper, a hard edge to his voice. 'It wouldn't be the first time, or the last.'

'You don't think she went off with some other man, do you?' said Darcy, disappointed at having her romantic scenario so prosaically flattened.

Cooper sighed. 'I think you should be writing plays, not acting in them! Do you always allow your imagination to run away with you like this?'

'I'm not imagining things,' she protested. 'A ring, letters, a torn photograph...how much more evidence do you need? And whatever happened, Uncle Bill was obviously broken-hearted.' She propped her chin in her hands with a sigh. 'It's so sad to think of him being in love with Violet all those years and never telling anyone. No wonder he never married!'

'He never married because he discovered he could manage perfectly well without the expense or complication of a wife,' said Cooper astringently. 'In fact, now that I look back on some of the things he said to me, I'd guess he thought he'd had a lucky escape.'

'He was probably just putting a brave face on things.'

Cooper was determined not to share her sense of tragedy. 'He always looked perfectly happy to me.'

He had looked perfectly happy when he had come to England, too, but Darcy chose to ignore that fact. 'He wouldn't tell *you* about it.'

'Why not? I was his partner. At the end of his life,
I probably knew him better than anyone.'

'You wouldn't understand his feelings,' she accused him.

'What makes you say that?'

'Well . . . you're obviously not in touch with your
emotions.'

At least she had succeeded in irritating him. 'I have
my emotions perfectly well under control, thank you!'

'Exactly!' Darcy pounced. 'They're too controlled.
You need to let your feelings find their own harmony.'

He looked at her incredulously. 'Do you learn this
rubbish at drama school?'

'It's not rubbish,' she said, offended. 'You'll end
up living on your own like Uncle Bill if you're not
careful.'

'I can think of worse fates, I can assure you!'

'I thought you wanted children?'

'Not if it means letting my feelings find their own
harmony!' said Cooper in disgust.

Darcy sat back in her chair with an air of finality.
'Well, I pity your poor wife, that's all I can say!'

'My wife will have too much to do to worry about
getting in touch with her emotions,' he said irritably.
'I suppose Sebastian is fully in touch with yours?'

'Sebastian is incredibly sensitive,' said Darcy.
Sebastian had always told her that he was, anyway,
although she had come to doubt whether he was sensitive to anyone's feelings but his own. Still, she had
told Cooper that she was still in love with Sebastian,
so she had better make sure he didn't forget it. 'Sometimes it feels as if we're just part of each other,' she
went on pointedly, hoping that it might make Cooper
feel bad about having kissed her.

Cooper looked more disgusted than guilty. 'I'm surprised you could bear to be parted from such a soul mate,' he sneered.

'Distance doesn't affect our relationship,' said Darcy quickly.

'It doesn't sound much of a relationship to me!'

'No, well, you *would* think that,' she said loftily. 'Sebastian and I have a wonderful relationship on both the physical and the spiritual plane.'

Cooper was finishing his coffee, studying her over the rim of his mug. 'In that case, why aren't you married?'

'Oh, we don't need to be tied by the bonds of convention,' said Darcy with assumed airiness.

'Is that another way of saying that you don't believe in marriage?'

'Yes . . . no . . . I mean, I do believe in marriage, but not unless everything's perfect.'

'But I thought Sebastian was,' said Cooper innocently.

'The circumstances aren't perfect,' she said, determinedly dignified. 'Sebastian has just got a leading role in a television costume drama. This could be the big break he's been waiting for, so we decided we would concentrate on our careers for the time being.'

'Coming out to Bindaburra seems an odd way to concentrate on your career,' he commented. 'Or has Sebastian decided that you'd be less distracting on the other side of the world?'

'Sebastian does not find me distracting!' Darcy snapped, getting to her feet and crossly gathering the plates and mugs together.

Cooper shook his head. 'Sebastian sounds like a very odd kind of man to me! What's the point of having a girl like you and not being distracted by her?'

'I'm not here to be distracting,' she said coldly.

'No,' he agreed, 'but you are anyway.'

CHAPTER FOUR

'IT's going to be a nice day.'

'How can you possibly tell?' said Darcy sourly, casting a jaundiced eye out of the window, where it was still dark. She couldn't remember a time when she had been up as early as this, and she was not enjoying it.

Why was she doing this to herself? she wondered morosely. She had spent all of yesterday afternoon blowing the dust off invoices and receipts dating back to the 1950s, and most of the evening trying to roast a huge piece of beef. It had not been a successful meal. Darcy had grown increasingly flustered as she'd wrestled with the old-fashioned stove, and by the time they'd sat down to eat, nearly two hours later than she had intended, she'd been hot and cross and mortified.

'I told you I wasn't a very good cook,' she had said defensively as Cooper had looked down at his plate with a telling lack of expression. 'And a kitchen that ought to be in a museum doesn't help! It hasn't even got a microwave!' For Darcy, who cooked almost exclusively by heating up prepared meals from the freezer, this was a major drawback. She had forgotten the art of cooking vegetables conventionally, as the unappetising display on her plate had borne eloquent witness.

'Perhaps we should get a cook in after all,' Cooper had said, also contemplating his dinner, but Darcy had bristled up at once. The dinner fiasco had only made her more determined to show him that she was good for more than scrubbing floors. Any cook they got in would no doubt be some sensible, practical girl with floury hands and a light touch with pastry who would only succeed in making Darcy look even more useless than Cooper thought her already, and Darcy wasn't having that. Besides, she wasn't going to give Cooper the opportunity of implying that she wasn't sticking to her half of the agreement and doing a partner's share of the work.

'We don't need a cook,' she said firmly. 'I was just having a few problems getting used to the kitchen. Breakfast will be better.'

Cooper looked at her sceptically. 'Are you really going to get up at five o'clock to cook breakfast?'

'Certainly,' said Darcy with bravado.

'Since the men aren't here, we could have breakfast a bit later if you like,' he offered, but his doubt only inflamed her resolve.

'No, if you usually have breakfast at five-thirty, that's when we'll have it.'

When her alarm had gone off at five o'clock this morning, Darcy had cursed herself for being so hasty. It was pitch-dark and freezing cold and the last thing she wanted to do was get out of her nice warm bed. Roused out of a deep sleep, she flailed one arm out of the bedclothes and groped around on the table for her alarm. This was usually a good technique for switching off the alarm and sinking back into sleep, but this morning her fumbling only succeeded in knocking the clock to the floor where, instead of breaking as it should rightfully have done, it lay and shrilled insistently until she was forced to get out of bed to pick it up.

She had spent part of yesterday afternoon going through her great-uncle's bedroom and had found, forgotten at the bottom of a drawer, a pair of fine cotton pyjamas, pale yellow and still unworn in their packet. Darcy had shaken them out. They were a little musty, perhaps, but clean and of such beautifully old-fashioned quality that they were almost stylish. They had certainly kept her warm last night, and she was glad of them as she pulled her dressing-gown around her. She didn't have time to shower and dress properly, and she hadn't welcomed the thought of appearing in front of Cooper dressed only in her robe again, not after what had happened yesterday!

Cooper looked amused when he saw her tying the dressing-gown tightly over the baggy pyjamas. She had taken the added precaution of buttoning the jacket up to the neck. 'I'm sure we could find a veil somewhere if you wanted to cover a little more of you!' he mocked.

Darcy looked up from the grill and glared at him, her sense of humour non-existent at this time of the morning. 'I didn't want a repetition of yesterday's incident,' she said grumpily. 'You were the one who wanted me to wear something less revealing!'

'I didn't say that was what I wanted,' said Cooper, pulling out a chair and sitting down at the kitchen table. He had showered and was looking revoltingly fresh and alert in a dark green shirt and jeans. 'I just said that it would be less distracting if you did.'

'Yes, well, I'd hate to distract you like that again,' snapped Darcy, then yelped as she burnt herself on the handle of the antiquated frying-pan. She shook her hand and sucked her finger, glaring at Cooper with accusing blue eyes. 'Now look what you've made me do!'

'What did I do?' he said with an air of surprise.

Darcy didn't have an immediate answer for this. The truth was that just having him in the same room made her nervous and clumsy, and trying to cook breakfast in the middle of the night didn't help matters.

'Surely I wasn't distracting you?' he went on, straight-faced, although the unsettling grey eyes were alight with amusement. He drew the collar of his shirt together with mock-modesty. 'Would you like me to go and put some more clothes on?'

'That won't be necessary,' said Darcy coldly. 'I don't find you the least bit distracting—not in that way anyway.'

She banged an egg on the edge of the frying-pan with such venom that it promptly smashed, half of it spilling into the pan, shell and all, and the other half oozing into an unpleasant mess on the element. Darcy muttered under her breath and scraped the pan clean to start again. The next egg all went into the pan, at least, but the yolk broke—but the second one was more successful. Darcy regarded it proudly, only to curse when she discovered that it had stuck to the pan. Her attempts to lift it out resulted in what could only be described as a smeary mess, but Darcy was so bad-tempered by this stage that she plonked it on top of the steak and banged the plate down in front of Cooper.

'Oh, good, scrambled egg!'

'There's no need to be smart!' she snapped, slumping down at the table and reaching for her coffee. 'I can't think how you can eat at this time of the morning anyway!'

Cooper picked up his knife and fork and gamely tackled his steak, which was cleverly charred around the edges. 'Is it going to be like this every morning?' he asked with a sigh.

'You can't expect me to turn into a cordon-bleu cook overnight!'

'I was thinking more about your temper,' he said without looking up from his breakfast. 'Are you always this cross at this time of day?'

'I wouldn't know. I've never been up at this time before!'

'Perhaps you'll get more cheerful as you get used to it.'

'What is there to be cheerful about?' grumbled Darcy, nursing her sore hand. 'I'm cold and tired and suffering from third-degree burns after cooking your rotten breakfast in that frying-pan!'

That was when Cooper told her it was going to be a nice day. 'It's not raining,' he said reasonably.

Darcy remained determinedly unconvinced, but by the time she had showered and dressed she saw with something of a shock that Cooper had been right. Shaded by the veranda, the house was still dim, but outside was a world she had never seen before.

The wet, dark gloom which had shrouded the house ever since she had arrived had vanished so utterly that it was as if it had never been, and Darcy blinked in disbelief at the scene which met her eyes.

The homestead was built on a slight rise, looking over the creek and beyond to the vast gibber plain stretching emptily towards the horizon, flat and stony and desolate. There was something magnificent in its

utter emptiness. The gums lining the creek were a thin
olive-green barrier between the water and the desert;
beyond them Darcy could see no trees, no bushes, not
a blade of green, only the faint metallic shimmer of
the stones in the sun and a line of red sand-dunes,
rising abruptly out of the plain in the distance, their
pure, curving lines a contrast to the flat, featureless
brown.

Around the homestead, the gums stood out in sharp
relief against the cloudless blue sky. Darcy's feet
crunched over the curls of dried bark that lay scattered beneath them as she walked down towards the
creek. It was high and fast still, swirling brown and
muddy around the pale trunks of the massive river
red gums that leant over the water.

The air was filled with the sound of birds, trilling
and crying and squawking and cheeping and twit-
tering. Darcy recognised the long, disappointed caw
of rooks, but it seemed odd and out of place when
there were parrots and budgerigars darting across the
water in flashes of yellow and blue and green. Suddenly a huge gum in front of her erupted in a wheeling
blur as hundreds of the white parrots called corellas
took off together and resettled, beating their wings
aggressively, and she clapped her hands over her ears
as they screeched in protest at her approach.

'All right, all right, I'm going,' she muttered, and
turned back to the homestead.

It was the first time she had seen Bindaburra from
the outside. The homestead was a long, low building
with a corrugated-iron roof that flashed in the sunlight, and surrounded on all sides by a wide veranda.
Clustered behind the house Darcy could see a collection of sturdy stone buildings and a huge old

woolshed which gave it the air of a small settlement. A windmill towering above the round water tanks turned slowly in the light breeze.

So this was Bindaburra. This was the place Uncle Bill had loved so much, the place Cooper wanted so badly for his own. Darcy walked slowly around the homestead. To her it looked like a plain house in need of new paint, clinging doggedly to the edge of an inhospitable environment. What was it about this place that meant so much to them?

She met Cooper coming back from checking the horses in the paddock. As soon as she saw him, Bindaburra and its jumbled collection of outhouses receded into the middle distance, fading with the gums and the noisy birds until there was only Cooper, quiet and tall and self-contained, walking towards her with that distinctively deliberate, easy stride. His hat shaded his eyes but the light just caught the cool, exciting line of his cheek and the stern mouth that could relax so intriguingly into a smile.

Of course, she hadn't had any breakfast, Darcy reminded herself. That would explain this odd hollow feeling, and the sudden weakness in her knees.

'Inspecting your property?' he asked as he came up.

Darcy dragged her eyes away from his mouth and nodded. 'I was just having a look around. I hadn't seen it before.'

'What do you think?'

Darcy looked around her, but was aware only of Cooper's lean, balanced strength beside her. 'It's not really what I was expecting,' she said at last.

'If it's any comfort, I don't think you're quite what Bindaburra was expecting.' His voice was deep and slow, and amusement creased the lines bracketing his mouth.

'I didn't think Bindaburra was expecting me at all,' she said, wishing she didn't sound so breathless.

'Exactly,' he said. 'It's survived fire and flood and drought, but it hasn't had to cope with anyone quite like you before.'

'I dare say it'll survive,' said Darcy, thinking that she hadn't had to cope with anyone like Cooper before either. 'Whether you'll survive my cooking or not is another matter!'

'I think it's more a question of surviving your dislike of early mornings.' He looked down at her standing slim and vibrant in the dust, one hand up to shade her eyes from the glare. 'You're much nicer now. You should try and be nice like this all the time.'

'I will if you will.'

'*I'm* not cross in the mornings,' Cooper pointed out virtuously.

'No, but you're not very nice either—at any time!'

'Why, what have I done?'

Darcy looked down at her feet. 'It's not so much what you've done, it's the way you say things. You don't smile, but I can tell that you're laughing at me underneath...' She trailed off, realising that she wasn't explaining herself very clearly. 'What I mean is that we should both try harder to be pleasant to each other,' she tried again. 'I know we don't have much in common, but we could at least try and be friends.'

Cooper studied her thoughtfully. 'You're not the kind of girl men usually want to be friends with, Darcy, but I'll try.'

They both tried. For the next four days they were carefully polite to each other. Darcy couldn't quite manage to be cheerful at breakfast, but she did make a huge effort not to snap, and for his part Cooper learnt only to talk to her when it was absolutely essential before the sun was well up.

It didn't take long to fall into a routine. Slowly, Darcy's cooking improved as she got used to the kitchen. She was still inclined to burn the steaks, but she learnt how to crack eggs and make biscuits and when on the fourth day she managed to bake a cake she was so proud of it that she could hardly bear to let Cooper eat it.

Tackling the housekeeping had been a matter of pride at first, but to her own surprise Darcy soon found that she was too busy to be bored. She cooked and cleaned, opened up rooms that had stood unused for years and cleared out cupboards. In the afternoons, they would continue sorting the papers in her great-uncle's office into some sort of order, leaving Cooper to decide what should be kept and what could be thrown away.

The evenings were the most difficult times. Cooper was out for most of the day, but he would come in about six o'clock, stamping the dust off his boots on the veranda steps and brushing off his hat as the screen door banged to behind him. Every time Darcy willed her heart not to react when his rangy figure appeared in the kitchen doorway, and every time it somersaulted up into her throat to thump back into place with a blow that took her breath away.

Sometimes she wished that she'd never suggested being friends. It had been easier when they had snapped at each other, easier to remember how much she disliked him. Now she spent the evenings feverishly trying to think of something to say that would take her mind off his cheek and his jaw, the way the lines starred underneath his eyes, the way the long brown fingers held his beer. Something that would stop her remembering how warm and sure those same hands had been against her skin and how it had felt to be held against him.

Whenever Darcy looked at Cooper's mouth, her stomach seemed to disappear in a wash of some dark, dangerous emotion that she preferred not to identify. It left her feeling restless and uneasy and dried the brittle flow of words on her tongue.

It was impossible to tell what Cooper felt. He was scrupulously polite, but Darcy sensed that he had himself under tightly leashed control, which only added to the simmering tension between them. He never touched her again, but their careful avoidance of any kind of physical contact only made things worse. They might be polite to each other, but they weren't friends.

Things were a little easier once the creek dropped far enough to enable the ringers to return from the out-station where they had spent a week working. Jim, Gary and Darren were all quiet, reserved men, inarticulately shy with Darcy, but their slow drawls made meals less of an ordeal. They would go back to their own quarters afterwards, though, and there was still the rest of the evening to be got through. The days were warm and sunny, but at night the temperature dropped dramatically, and Darcy would light a fire in the sitting-room. Cooper would sit in a big high-backed chair and read, and Darcy would try to do the same, but she never got beyond the sixth page. The book would lie open on her lap, while her eyes kept sliding away from the print to watch him cov-

ertly under her lashes until he looked up and she had
to bend her head hurriedly over the page again.

As the days passed, the politeness between them
became increasingly strained, until it snapped
altogether one day as they were moving the last of the
sorted papers into the new office. The room which
had seemed so much bigger when they had chosen it
seemed to have shrunk with the addition of the desk
and two filing cabinets, and it was impossible to avoid
brushing against each other in the confined space.
Every time they touched, Darcy felt a *frisson* that
screwed the tension a notch higher.

Like most rows, it started over something quite
trivial. Darcy had a big pile of invoices in her hands
and was leaning down to put them in the middle
drawer of one of the filing cabinets just as Cooper
straightened from where he had been crouching by
the other. Their shoulders just grazed each other, but
Darcy jerked instinctively away as if she had been
stung and lost her grip on the invoices, which cas-
caded to the floor.

'Now look what you've done!' said Cooper, irritation getting the better of him. 'I spent all yesterday
evening sorting those into date order! Can't you be
more careful?'

'I wouldn't have dropped them if you hadn't shoved
me like that!' Guilt made Darcy sound peevish as she
dropped to her knees to gather the invoices together.

'*Shoved* you?' Cooper gazed down at her incredulously. 'I hardly touched you!'

'It might have felt that way to you, but to me it felt
like being rammed by a ten-ton truck!'

'Don't be ridiculous!' He crouched down to help
her collect the invoices, which had scattered all over

the floor. 'Why do you always have to be so melodramatic about everything?'

'I am not being melodramatic!'

'Yes, you are. You exaggerate everything. It's never
cool, it's always freezing, a slight shower is a deluge.
It's never early, it's always the middle of the night; if
you cut yourself, you're handicapped for life. I'd
suggest you tried to be more moderate about things,
but, knowing you, you'd take moderation to
extremes!'

It had taken only seconds for the veneer of politeness to shatter completely. Darcy was grabbing invoices, careless of the fact that they were crumpling
as she slapped them together. 'It's not my fault if
you're so boring that you can't cope with anyone
different!'

'Of course, you would think that anyone who
doesn't carry on like you would be boring!' Cooper's
eyes were cold and his mouth was set in a tight, angry
line. 'I'm sure that pretentious actressy act goes down
well with your precious Sebastian, but it doesn't impress me.'

'Nothing would impress you!'

'I'd be impressed if I thought you were making an
effort learning how to behave appropriately.'

'I don't need you to tell me how to behave!' said
Darcy furiously, blue eyes flashing dangerously. 'In
case you'd forgotten, half of Bindaburra belongs to
me, and I can behave exactly how I like.'

Cooper gave an exclamation of impatience and
thrust a handful of the invoices he had gathered at
Darcy, who snatched them away and slammed them
down on her pile. 'How much longer are you going
to persist with this stupid idea?' he demanded. 'You

don't belong here, and it's obvious that you're bored stiff. If you don't like it, why don't you just give up and go home?'

'You'd like that, wouldn't you?' she said, the built-up tension releasing itself in a satisfying surge of fury. 'You've done everything you possibly can to make me go! I can't believe I really fell for all that rubbish about a truce when it was just a way of saving yourself the expense of a cook for as long as it took you to bully me into going!' She pushed her hair angrily away from her face and swung round to face him with blazing eyes. 'Well, I'm sick of getting up in the middle of the night—sorry, *early*—to cook your disgusting breakfast. I'm sick of washing up and scrubbing floors and peeling vegetables . . . and I'm sick of picking up stupid bits of paper, too!' Scooping up the pile she had just gathered together, Darcy threw it high into the air and scrambled to her feet through the fluttering invoices. 'But if you think that means I'm giving up and going home, you've got another think coming! It just means you can pick up your own invoices,' she finished, and stalked towards the door.

'Where are you going?' A muscle was hammering in Cooper's cheek.

'Out.'

'Out where?'

'Out on to my own property,' said Darcy with emphasis. 'Not that it's any of your business!'

'It'll be my business if you get lost!'

She turned at the door, vivid with anger. 'I'm not going to get lost,' she told him bitingly. 'I'm not entirely stupid, and, since it's my land, I'll go wherever I choose!'

Slamming the door behind her, she marched down the corridor towards the veranda. Sheer rage carried her clattering down the steps and out to the creek. It was a familiar sight by now, and Darcy had fallen into the habit of walking down there at sunset before the men came in for their meal, but the creek had no power to soothe her this afternoon. She would have to walk her rage out of her system.

Darcy hesitated only a second before swinging round and heading left, following the line of the creek. The water level had receded and the turbulent swirl that she had first seen might never have been. Instead the huge white branches of the gums were mirrored in the still water. Red mulgas and paper bark trees clustered between the gums along the edge of the creek and Darcy had to make her way carefully along the steep edge, climbing over the bleached dead branches and clumps of dry, tangled shrubs. Sometimes there would be a narrow beach to walk along, but the going was too slow for her mood, and she set off at a tangent. Away from the creek, the magnificent trees gave way to sparser gums, and she swung along between them, hardly noticing where she was going as Cooper's words circled around and around in her head. 'You don't belong here.'

He hated her and her 'pretentious, actressy' ways. Well, let him! To her fury, Darcy found that she was crying, and she brushed the tears angrily from her cheeks. At the end of some of those long, tense evenings, she had begun to consider leaving, but she definitely wasn't going now!

Darcy walked on, heedless of the trees growing sparser and more spindly until they were little more than bushes, only stopping in surprise when the vegetation stopped abruptly. Beyond was an undulating stony plane, rising up to a low, flat-topped hill. It didn't look too far, and Darcy was still too angry to turn around and go tamely back to the homestead, where Cooper would probably just accuse her of being extreme again.

Mindful of her claim that she wouldn't get lost, Darcy made a note of a distinctive dead tree. Its blackened branches pointed in a V to the sky; she would be able to see it from the top of the hill easily, and then she would just have to retrace her steps to the creek. Easy.

By the time she got to the top of the hill, Darcy was hot and panting. The hill had been further and steeper than she had realised, but the strenuous exercise had cleared her mind, and she felt calmer as she found a low flat stone to sit on and looked about her. On one side, the creek was hidden in the distance by the ribbon of grey-green trees; on the other was the horizon. In between, the stones that made up the gibber plain had assumed a metallic glint in the sun.

It was like sitting in a rocky moonscape where the only colour was the burningly blue sky above the monotonous reddish-brown of the gibber and the only sound was the buzzing of the flies that had followed her out from the trees. Why would anyone want to live in this barren place? Darcy rested her arms on her knees. Come to that, what was *she* doing here? Why didn't she do as Cooper suggested and simply go home to a world she knew?

Darcy thought about her life in London, about the flat she shared with a friend, the lunches and the parties and the whole gossipy, incestuous theatre world. It had been her whole life before she came to

Bindaburra; now it seemed impossibly remote. Darcy couldn't even imagine herself there any more, and wondered gloomily if she was destined not to belong anywhere.

Most unnerving of all was the fact that she could no longer picture Sebastian clearly. The beat of her heart for nine months, he was now no more than a hazy memory. Darcy closed her eyes and tried to concentrate, but it was Cooper's face that refused to be banished. It was a shock to realise just how clearly she could visualise him. She knew the exact angle of his cheek and brow, knew just how the hair grew from his forehead and how his mouth curved into something that was almost, but not quite, a smile. She could probably count every crease at the edges of his eyes, Darcy thought, and was hit by an unexpected wave of intense loneliness not to have him there.

She stood up. She didn't know what she was going to say when she got back to the homestead, but suddenly she wanted to be there more than anything.

It was then that she realised just how many dead trees with V-shaped branches there were bordering the edge of the gibber. Which one was hers?

A shiver of foreboding slid down her spine, but she forced herself not to panic, and set off down the hill in what seemed like the right direction. The very sameness of the landscape was disorientating, and when she got to the trees every direction seemed the same. The creek had to be in front of her, she reasoned, but it wasn't long before she began to wonder if she was walking as straight as she thought she was. Surely she should have hit the creek by now?

If only she hadn't been too angry to keep any track of time! Darcy faltered to a halt as she realised that she had no idea how far she had walked in her fury. Nothing looked familiar. Instead the trees had assumed an alien air, and the silence was suddenly heavy and sinister. Darcy would even have welcomed the harsh screech of the corellas that congregated in the river red gums, but there was nothing. Even the flies seemed to have abandoned her.

'I'm not going to get lost'. Wasn't that what she had told Cooper so confidently?

Darcy could feel the beginnings of panic clawing at her spine. Would she ever find her way back to Bindaburra, or was she doomed to wander helplessly round in circles out here? Cooper might never find her. Her father had warned her not to come out here on her own; what would he feel when he heard that she was missing? Darcy's eyes began to fill with tears as she pictured her parents' distress until Cooper's image intervened and she could almost hear his stringent tones telling her not to be so melodramatic.

For some reason, the thought of him steadied her. Standing quite still, she orientated herself and decided that she had been walking in quite the wrong direction. The creek must be somewhere to her right. It took her some time, but she found it just as she was beginning to think that she must have been right the first time. She had come much further than she had realised. The creek was much narrower here, and edged by huge, eerie black boulders worn smooth by time. Others were a strange rusty red and cracked into almost geometric shapes, watched over by the stark skeletons of dead trees that were bleached white by the sun. A lizard froze at Darcy's approach then vanished down a crack with a flick of its tail.

She shivered. There was something uncanny about this place. The silence hung heavy and intense, almost as if it was waiting for something. Darcy's instinct was to back away, but she would have to cross the rocks if she wanted to get back to the creek. In her hurry to leave them behind, she slipped and her foot turned over painfully between two boulders.

At least she hadn't broken her ankle, Darcy thought, limping along the creek. This was one place she would *not* want to be stuck on her own. It was a relief when the rocks gave way to the blessedly familiar gum trees once more, but it was slow going on her sore foot and by the time she finally glimpsed Bindaburra ahead it was almost dark, the water glowing dully red in the last blaze of sunset. Darcy didn't notice as she struggled along through spiky bushes, stumbling and slipping until she was ready to weep with exhaustion.

Limping up the creek towards the homestead, she saw through the gloom that the men were all standing in conference on the veranda.

Suddenly one of them spotted her, and they all turned. Even in the dim light, Darcy recognised Cooper in the middle of the group, his lean body taut with tension as he stepped forward, dismissing the other men with a murmur. They melted away into the shadows and Darcy and Cooper were left alone, facing each other through the dusk.

He was very angry. Darcy could feel his fury from where she hesitated at the bottom of the steps, but he said nothing, only watched her with cold, cold eyes as she wearily climbed the veranda steps.

'Where have you been?' He didn't raise his voice, but Darcy felt as if she had been struck by a lash.

'I've just had the men here ready to come out and look for you! I can't believe that even you could be so stupid and irresponsible as to stay out until dark in unfamiliar country! Did it ever occur to you that I might be worried? That others would have to go out and look for you in the dark after a hard day's work? Or even that they would have to do without their meal since you couldn't be bothered to come back in time to prepare it?'

Darcy opened her mouth to defend herself, but found that she couldn't say anything. White-faced, she could only stare back at him, and fight the tears of reaction that tightened a band of steel around her throat.

Cooper watched her bite down hard on her lower lip to steady her treacherously wobbling mouth. Opening his mouth to say something blistering, he changed his mind and reached for her instead, pulling her hard against him so that Darcy could bury her dark head in his shoulder and burst into over-wrought tears.

CHAPTER FIVE

COOPER'S body was strong, wonderfully solid. Darcy clung to him, ashamed of her tears but immensely grateful for the safety of his arms. 'I'm s-sorry,' she wept. 'I'm so sorry...'

'Are you hurt?' His voice was rough but she could hear the concern in it, and she shook her head.

'N-no.'

'Darcy, where have you been?' Cooper sounded torn between exasperation and concern.

'I don't know,' said Darcy tearfully, her voice muffled by his shoulder. 'I went too far, and I was too angry to look where I was going. I couldn't find my way back.' She shuddered at the memory and clung tighter. 'I thought I knew where the creek was, but I walked and walked and I must have been going in completely the wrong direction. I thought I was never going to get back,' she went on, drawing a jagged breath. 'Everything was so strange. I didn't know where I was, or what I was doing. You were right— I just don't belong here.'

Cooper sighed. 'I was just in a bad mood, Darcy. You must have known that I didn't mean half the things I said.'

'You meant that,' said Darcy, still muffled.

'All right, I'm sorry,' he said. 'I lost my temper and took it out on you. I was going to apologise when we got home, but you weren't here. I've been frantic with worry thinking about what might have happened to you, and blaming myself for letting you go off in such a state.'

'It wasn't your fault,' she muttered. Her tears had dried to a few hiccuping breaths, but she was curiously reluctant to move from the comfort of his arms. 'I over-reacted, just as I always do. You were right about that, too. I hate the way you're right about everything,' she added, sounding so much more like her usual self that she felt Cooper smile.

'Things have been a little strained recently, haven't they?'

'It was easier when we weren't being polite to each other.' His rock-like solidity and steady breathing had calmed Darcy down, but she was now too assailed by shyness to move away. What on earth had possessed her to burst into childish tears like that?

'That's easily solved,' said Cooper with an undercurrent of amusement. 'Let's simply agree not to be polite to each other any more.'

'All right,' said Darcy indistinctly. She half expected him to push her away, but he almost seemed to have forgotten that he was holding her at all. He had rested his chin on her tousled hair and was smoothing a hand absently up and down her spine as if soothing a nervous animal. Darcy felt herself relaxing dangerously. Her fingers trembled with the desire to explore the broad, muscular back that she had clung to so desperately at first, and as the fear and the tension and the tiredness drained away her mind became obsessed with the knowledge that if she turned her head just slightly she would be able to rest her face against the strong column of his throat. She would be able to touch her lips to his skin, to taste him, to breathe in the warm, masculine scent of him. And then if *he* brought his face down to hers ...

It was nearly dark. The corellas had settled at last in the trees and the air was cold and quiet. For Darcy, the world had shrunk to the slow thud of her heart and the feel of Cooper breathing against her. It felt so safe in his arms, so. warm, so *right*.

'Better now?' he asked, as if suddenly recollecting where he was and what he was doing with Darcy in his arms.

She nodded reluctantly, and he slid his hands to her waist to put her gently from him. She felt like a limpet being prised from its rock, and she wrapped her arms about herself against the cold, unable to meet Cooper's eyes.

There was an awkward silence. 'Well, who's going to be rude first?' said Cooper, a curious note in his voice.

'I don't feel like being very rude at the moment,' Darcy confessed, looking down at her shoes.

'You must be feeling bad!'

She shook her head, and wiped the tear-stains away with a knuckle. 'I just feel stupid.'

'Come on, you're cold,' said Cooper with brusque sympathy. 'You'd better get inside.' He held open the screen door for her, frowning as he saw Darcy limp. 'What have you done to your ankle?'

She told him about the rocks she had come across. 'You've walked all the way back from *there* with a sprained ankle?' he said in disbelief. 'How did you get that far?'

'I don't know,' she said honestly. 'I only know that I feel as if I've seen enough of the outback to last me a lifetime!'

'You haven't seen the country properly,' said Cooper as he let the door bang shut behind him. 'I think it's time I showed you the real Bindaburra. It sounds as if you could do with a break from the kitchen, and the men can manage by themselves for a couple of days. I'll take you out tomorrow and show you just what you've inherited.'

'Do we have to walk?' said Darcy cautiously. After this afternoon, she wasn't sure that she wanted to see any more of Bindaburra.

Cooper's smile gleamed through the gloom. 'We wouldn't see very much of Bindaburra if we walked,' he said. 'Especially not if you've got a sore ankle. Can you ride?'

'No,' she said firmly. She had tried riding once— never again! She was aching enough as it was.

'In that case we'll take the ute,' said Cooper, then hesitated. 'If you'd like to go, that is. You can stay here if you'd rather.'

Darcy stopped, appalled by the discovery that she didn't care where she was, as long as he was there too. Glad of the darkness of the corridor that hid her expression, she drew a deep, steadying breath. 'No, I'd like to go,' she said.

They left after breakfast the next morning with the sun still low on the horizon. Darcy was quiet, chastened by the previous day's experience and disturbed by the depth of her new feelings for Cooper. She couldn't stop thinking about how safe it had felt in his arms. Over and over again she had told herself that it was just reaction to the fear of finding herself lost, but that didn't explain the frightening urge she had had to turn and touch her lips to his skin. Darcy

had tried everything to deny it to herself, but in the
depths of the night she had admitted the truth.

She had wanted Cooper to kiss her.

She had wanted it very badly.

Now she sat beside him in the ute and told herself
that she would feel differently in the cold light of day.
It was impossible to believe that it was less than two
weeks since she had sat in this seat for the first time.
It seemed a lifetime ago, before Cooper had become
the focus of her life. Had there really been a time
when she hadn't known him, hadn't known how
strong and sure his hands could be, how warm his
lips?

Darcy wrenched her attention back to the present
as they rattled over the cattle-grid, and concentrated
fiercely on the scenery instead.

As he had promised, Cooper showed a very different Bindaburra from the one she had seen yesterday. Or did she just see things differently because
she was with him? They bumped for miles along rough
tracks across the vast stretch of gibber plain, but what
had been a desolate brown emptiness was today an
awe-inspiring vista of space and light. The sky was
huge, a deep, glaring blue, and the sun glinted on the
sharp edges of the stones. Where Darcy had seen only
a lifeless desert, Cooper showed her the tiny, exquisite
wild flowers between the rocks and enthused over the
blue-green haze of saltbush that grew after the rains
and fed the cattle who browsed in scattered groups,
stoical brown and white beasts with gentle eyes.
Cooper would stop the ute and point out a particularly fine calf or heifer, and Darcy would nod wisely
and try not to notice how the shadow of his hat fell
over his face. Whenever she looked at him he seemed

to be silhouetted against the long, empty horizon,
every detail about him sharply defined in the daz-
zlingly clear light. The buttons on his shirt, the
stitching on his jeans, the dull felt of his hat and the
dark hairs on his forearms all struck Darcy with a
peculiar sense of immediacy.

They had lunch sitting high on top of a dune. From
a distance, the dunes looked like low red bumps
floating above the horizon, and Darcy was unprepared for their magnificent size. Anchored on their
lower flanks by clumps of spinifex and canegrass and
drifts of yellow daisies and wild white stocks, the
dunes soared up into the sky, so that when Darcy stood
at the bottom and looked up all she could see was a
sweeping line dividing the blue from the deep, orange-
red sand.

Their feet slid back through the sand as they
climbed, and Darcy was breathless by the time they
reached the top. Cooper made her turn slowly until
she had seen the whole circular horizon. 'That's all
Bindaburra,' he told her proudly.

'Bindaburra means a lot to you, doesn't it?' she
said.

He stretched out on the sand and propped himself
up on one elbow, his eyes on the distant horizon. 'I
grew up on stories about Bindaburra and how hard
they had to work just to survive,' he told her.
'Bindaburra was always special. My father built up
another property after my grandfather had to sell out,
but it was never the same. He couldn't bear the fact
that Bill ran Bindaburra instead of him. They had
been good friends once, but there was some quarrel,
long before I was born, and he and Bill never spoke
after that. They were both hard, stubborn men.'

Cooper shook his head, remembering. 'My father used to long for a sight of the creek at Bindaburra, but he would never swallow his pride and make it up with Bill so that he could come here again.'

'Do you want Bindaburra for your father's sake or for your own?' asked Darcy.

'Both,' said Cooper. 'This was once one of the finest properties in Australia, and I'm going to make it so again. Bill loved Bindaburra as much as any Anderson, but he didn't have enough money to invest and keep it thriving. I do.'

Darcy sat next to him on the soft sand and looked out over Bindaburra. She would never feel about it the way he did, but now, for the first time, she thought she had an inkling of what it must feel like to belong here. Cooper had made her wear her uncle's battered old hat, but the light breeze kept the temperature down to that of a perfect English summer's day. Darcy could feel the sun warm on her back as she trickled the fine sand through her fingers, and a queer, quiet exhilaration spread through her to be sitting there surrounded by light, with only the sound of the wind and the occasional piping call of a bird to disturb the silence and Cooper beside her, his profile etched in sharp relief against the indigo sky.

The tingling happiness stayed with her all afternoon as they drove along dusty tracks and splashed through the recent rain that still lay gathered in shrinking pools along the creek beds until they came at last to a long, deep waterhole that was part of the same creek that ran past the homestead a day's drive away. The stately gums and the darting birds and the still water were all as familiar to Darcy now as the red double-decker buses and ticking taxis of London had been before.

She stretched as she climbed out of the ute and plucked at her shirt. She was hot and sticky and in spite of its light muddy brown colour the creek looked cool and inviting. 'Do you get crocodiles here?'

'Crocs?' Cooper looked up from unloading the back of the ute. 'No, this is fresh water here. Why?'

Darcy took the spade he handed her and propped it against the wheel. 'I thought I might have a swim.'

'I don't recommend it,' said Cooper. 'The water's cold.'

'I'm English,' she reminded him. 'I'm used to swimming in cold water.'

'You'd be better off having a wash in this,' he said, tossing her a red plastic bucket. 'That's what I do. If you wait till I get the fire going, I could even heat up some water in the billy for you.'

'I'd rather have a swim,' Darcy decided.

Cooper grinned, rather suspiciously, she thought. 'Suit yourself, but the offer still stands if you change your mind.'

'I won't,' she told him defiantly. 'We English are tougher than you think!'

She hadn't thought to bring a swimsuit with her, and, although she would have loved simply to take everything off, the thought of Cooper's eyes on her made her pull on a T-shirt over her pants.

A natural platform where gnarled tree roots had been filled with dusty sand and dried gum leaves stuck out at the bottom of the creek bank. As Darcy slithered gingerly down, she saw Cooper scooping up a bucketful of water. He had stripped to the waist, and her eyes lingered on his smooth, broad brown back, watching the muscles rippling as he lifted the bucket from the water and straightened.

Turning at her approach, she saw his gaze in its turn rest on her slender legs. Darcy had to resist the desire to tug the T-shirt down over her thighs, and assumed an air of unconcern as she dipped a toe in the water.

It was more than cold. It was glacial.

'Sure you don't want to change your mind?' asked Cooper, who must have seen her involuntary flinch, judging by the ripple of amusement in his voice.

'Change my mind?' said Darcy bravely. 'Certainly not! I've got the honour of England to think of!'

She plunged in before she had time to think better of it. The water was very deep, and it closed such an icy hand around her heart that for a ghastly moment Darcy was afraid that she was simply going to stop breathing. At first she could only flail around, gasping frantically, the cold so intense that she couldn't manage any kind of coherent action.

On the bank, Cooper was sluicing himself with water. He grinned at Darcy. 'What's it like in there?' he called.

'Lovely,' she managed to gasp, determined not to give him the satisfaction of admitting that he had been right yet again. 'Very refreshing!'

Pride forced her to stay in the water until Cooper had finished washing and was rubbing his hair with a towel, but she was so cold by then that she was glad of his hand to haul her up on to the bank.

'All right, I give in,' said Cooper, throwing the towel round her shoulders and rubbing her briskly. 'I take back everything I implied about you not being tough! I didn't think you'd last ten seconds in there!'

'It felt like ten hours,' confessed Darcy with some difficulty through clattering teeth. She was still shivering violently, but Cooper's vigorous rubbing was inducing a warm glow inside her. She was very conscious of his bare chest and had to clutch the towel around her to stop herself reaching out to touch him.

Afterwards, she sat on a log and combed out her wet hair while Cooper made some tea. Lifting the billycan off the fire, he threw in some tea-leaves and set it near the flames to brew.

Now that she was warm and dry once more, Darcy felt alive and invigorated, as if all her perceptions had been refreshed by the swim as well. The air was sharp and clean, edged with the tang of the dried gum leaves underfoot and the smell of the smoke curling slowly upwards from the fire. Overhead, the corellas screeched and squabbled in the branches and the rooks called mournfully to each other, while a solitary pelican cruised along the creek in dignified silence.

'It's beautiful here,' she sighed as Cooper tapped the side of the billy with a stick to settle the leaves and poured the tea into two enamel mugs. 'I didn't realise it could be like this.'

'It's like this at the homestead too,' he pointed out, handing her a mug.

Darcy took it and blew softly on the hot tea. 'I know, but I never saw it like this before. I suppose I was always thinking about what to make for smoko, or wondering if something was burning in the oven.' In fact, she had spent most of her time down by the creek thinking about Cooper himself, but she didn't think she would tell him that.

'Poor Darcy!' Cooper sat down beside her on the log, but was careful not to touch her. 'I don't suppose you spend much time thinking about what to cook for smoko at home?'

'No,' said Darcy slowly. Her life in London seemed strangely distant, like something she had once seen in a film. Sipping her tea, she looked out across the creek. It was glassy still, rippled only by the occasional plop of a fish jumping, and reflecting the deep blue of the sky as the afternoon light burnished everything with gold.

'It must be very dull for you here.' There was an unusually strained note in Cooper's voice. 'Cooking and cleaning isn't very exciting compared to being an actress in London. I'd have thought you'd have been desperate to get back to a more glamorous lifestyle.'

'Everyone thinks being an actress must be glamorous, but it isn't really,' she said. 'Oh, it's wonderful if you're involved in a good production, and there's a real thrill in just being on stage, but I spend most of my time sitting by the phone waiting for my agent to ring, or trailing round auditions, and if I'm not doing that I'm standing for hours on the set of some soap opera, waiting to be called as an extra. In fact,' she finished, as if it was the first time the thought had occurred to her, 'a lot of it's really very boring.'

Cooper looked at her in surprise. 'I imagined you fighting your way through your fans to the stage door and being swept off to nightclubs after another wildly successful performance.'

'That's how I like to imagine myself too,' said Darcy, slightly shamefaced. 'I pretend I'm a famous actress, but it's not true at all. The nearest I got to a decent part was in a play that folded after two weeks.' She looked down at her tea, remembering how scathing the critics had been. 'I was absolutely awful.'

'You surprise me,' said Cooper, studying her averted profile. 'I would have said that, if nothing else, you had the sort of star quality that would stand out in any crowd.'

Darcy shook her head. 'I'm good at all the carrying on and being an actress, but the truth is that I'm not very good at acting. My agent once told me that I wasted my dramatic talent off-stage. It's a wonder I ever got to drama school at all, really, but I loved it. My father wanted me to do something useful like a secretarial course, but I don't think I'd have been a very good secretary.'

A smile tugged at the corner of Cooper's mouth. 'I can't see you being that sensible,' he agreed.

'I badgered my parents until they gave in,' she told him. 'I'd love to get a good role, if only to show them that it was all worth it, but as it is I have to support myself waitressing between roles.'

'Waitresses can't usually afford to jump on planes to Australia,' Cooper commented.

'My father lent me the fare, remember?' said Darcy. 'He said that I should come and see Bindaburra as Uncle Bill wanted before I made any decisions. The play had just folded and there was nothing else in the offing, so I just got on the first plane I could and came. To be quite honest, I was glad to get away. It was obvious that I was never going to be a big star, and I needed some time to think.'

The sun was sinking in a glory of red and gold, turning the white bark of the ghost gums a delicate pink. In silence they watched two pelicans gliding low over the creek. Every now and then they would dip until they almost touched the water before a single beat of their wings would lift them back into their stately progress.

'At least Sebastian thinks you're a star,' said Cooper almost reluctantly when the pelicans had passed.

'No, Sebastian's the star,' Darcy said in a low voice. 'At least he will be. He really *is* a good actor.' She paused, apparently absorbed in clearing a space among the dried leaves with her shoe. 'I don't know why I told you he was still in love with me. It was silly of me. I—I suppose I didn't want to accept that he didn't love me any more.'

There was a silence. To her relief, Cooper didn't look at her. Instead he stirred a log on the fire with his foot. 'What happened?'

'Oh, the usual. Sebastian landed a part in a glossy new television series and started to move in more exalted circles. Suddenly he was on first-name basis with the stars, and I didn't fit his image any more.' She swallowed. 'What hurt most was that a friend had to tell me that he was having an affair with one of his co-stars. He didn't even have the decency to tell me himself. When I taxed him with it, he made a joke of it and pretended that it was just part of the game. He said it didn't mean anything, but that just made it worse as far as I was concerned.'

'You still felt betrayed and humiliated?'

'Yes.' The circle at her feet was getting bigger and bigger. 'Sebastian had a reputation before we got together, and all my friends warned me against him, but I wouldn't listen. I was so sure that he thought I was different, special, that I'd be the one to tame him. I told everyone that I'd prove them wrong, and I hated having to admit that they'd been right after all.' Darcy fell silent for a moment, remembering those bitter days. 'Yes, betrayed and humiliated. That's exactly how I felt.' She glanced at Cooper. 'How did you know?'

'It happens to the best of us,' he said with a twisted smile.

The thought that he had been in love with another girl made Darcy's heart twist. What sort of girl had she been, this girl who had been loved by him and who had betrayed him as he implied? Was he still in love with her?

She looked into the fire. 'Is that why you've never married?'

'Partly. Like Bill, I felt I'd had a lucky escape.'

'So you're not still in love with her?' Darcy asked the flames.

'No.' She could feel his gaze on her. 'Are you still in love with Sebastian?'

Very slowly, Darcy lifted her eyes to meet his. 'No,' she said. 'Not any more.'

As the darkness settled over them, Darcy huddled closer to the fire. She was wearing both the jumpers she had brought with her, but the cold crept down her neck and up her spine. Seeing her shiver, Cooper went to the ute and came back holding a thick woollen sweater.

'Here, put this on,' he said. 'I didn't think you'd have anything warm enough, so I brought one of mine for you.'

Darcy pulled it on over her jumpers gratefully. It was wonderfully warm and long, and she didn't care that she was so bulky that she could hardly move.

'It's not exactly the last word in fashion, but at least it should keep you warm,' he said, eyeing her critically.

'It's fine, thank you.' Darcy was suddenly, unaccountably shy. She smoothed down the sweater, unable to stop imagining it over Cooper's lean, hard body. It made her feel the same mixture of reassurance, alarm and confused yearning that she had felt with his arms about her.

Cooper barbecued some steaks on a hot plate over the glowing coals, and they ate in the flickering light of the fire he built up again afterwards. Darcy wasn't very hungry. She kept thinking about the warmth and comfort of the sweater and how much warmer and more comforting it would be with his arms around her.

Together they watched the moon rise with astonishing speed, silhouetting a tree against its huge squashed yellow gold globe as it slid up through the moonglow on the horizon to climb up into the dark sky, growing smaller and rounder and clearer as it went.

Outside the circle of firelight it was very dark. Darcy was preternaturally conscious of the smooth log beneath her thighs, of the smell of the smoke and the guttering sound of the flames that threw leaping shadows over Cooper's face. She watched him as he hunkered down by the fire to boil the billy, and as he turned his head to glance up at her her heart turned over with a sudden, terrible knowledge.

She was in love with him.

This wasn't the breathless infatuation she had had for Sebastian. This was need and desire and the instinctive recognition that here by the dark, still creek she had found the other half of herself.

Darcy was shaken by the depth of her certainty. She didn't know how she had fallen in love with

Cooper, or why. She only knew that he was a part of her now, that he had been ever since that first night when she had paused in the doorway to the kitchen, looking at him, and felt the extraordinary wash of recognition.

'You're very quiet.' Cooper's voice startled Darcy out of her thoughts. 'What are you thinking about?'

About you. About how much I love you. About how much I want you to draw me down off this log and lay me down beside you on the hard ground. I want to wrap myself around you and feel your hands against my skin, your mouth on mine. I want you to hold me and touch me and love me. I want you to tell me you'll never let me go.

Darcy didn't have the nerve to tell him the truth.

'I . . . I was just wishing Uncle Bill could be here,' she lied.

Cooper fed another log on to the fire. 'He would be glad to know that you came.'

'It doesn't seem right that you knew him better than I did,' said Darcy, twisting a leaf between her fingers. Could she tell Cooper that she was in love with him? *Could* she?

'I don't think anyone knew Bill well. I only knew him in the last year and a half. I told you that he and my father wouldn't have anything to do with each other, so I never really met him until my father died and we became partners. It was only then that I realised what a fine man he was.' He paused, poking the coals with a stick. 'He thought the world of you, though.'

'If you know that he thought that, don't you think he might have wanted me to have Bindaburra after all?'

Cooper threw the stick on the coals and stood up.
'No,' he said. 'I'm sorry, Darcy, but Bill didn't want
that. He wanted me to have it.'

Darcy wished she hadn't mentioned her inheritance. If she hadn't been so desperate not to blurt
out how much she loved him, she would have let the
issue lie, but now it lay between them again. She had
forgotten that she was a threat to Cooper's future.
He believed that Bindaburra should be his entirely,
and that wouldn't happen until she left.

How could she stay, knowing that he wanted her
to go?

How could she go, knowing that she would never
see him again?

Darcy lay rolled up in her bed-roll and stared up
at the night sky. She had never seen so many stars.
They were so bright and so numerous that the
blackness seemed to be covered with a blurry white
veil, and the Milky Way stretched in a luminous swath
right across the sky, beautiful, brilliant but impossibly remote and uncaring of her despair. The
moon was high and silver now. Darcy could see its
reflection shining on the still surface of the creek.

Cooper lay a few yards away, the white trunks of
the gums looming ghostly behind him. It was impossible to tell whether he was asleep or not, but his
quietly breathing presence was infinitely reassuring.

Why did he have to be the one? Why couldn't it
have been someone more like Sebastian whose world
she could share? Someone for whom she wasn't simply
a temporary difficulty? Someone who would want to
love her and care for her, who wouldn't leave her to
lie here on her own beneath the stars.

Far, far above her, a shooting star dropped through the night. Darcy closed her eyes for a wish. She knew that she ought to wish that she could wake up and discover that she wasn't in love with Cooper after all, but her heart wished something different. She wished that Cooper would roll over and hold out his arms with a smile. She wished that he would draw her down beside him and love her in the moonlight, that she could run her hands over his skin and bury into the hard security of his body.

A dingo howled in the distance and for one breathless moment Darcy thought that wishes came true after all. Cooper turned his head to look at her across the dying embers of the fire. She lay absolutely still. Let him smile, she prayed. Let him reach out his hand for me. Let him pull me down into his arms.

But he only raised himself slightly on one elbow. 'Are you all right?' he asked quietly.

Disappointment tightened Darcy's throat. 'I'm fine,' she said in a constricted voice.

'Not too cold?'

'No.'

She had the impression that Cooper was about to say something, but in the end he just lay down again and the silence closed between them.

Why hadn't she said anything? Darcy turned her back to him and told herself that it was better this way. She couldn't stay in Australia forever, and it was patently obvious that Cooper didn't feel the same way about her. Why make a fool of herself in front of him when it would be much easier for them both if they just carried on as before for the short time that remained? Wouldn't it be easier to leave with her pride intact?

It would, she decided, but it didn't make it any easier now. She had lied when she'd told Cooper that she felt fine. She didn't feel fine at all.

CHAPTER SIX

LOVE wasn't supposed to make you miserable, Darcy thought dolefully as they drove back to the homestead the next day. Yesterday's tingling happiness had faded, leaving her instead with a hollow sense of despair.

Cooper continued to explain how Bindaburra was run and Darcy forced herself to continue to sound interested, but although neither acknowledged it both were conscious of the new strain in the atmosphere. Darcy was torn between longing for the trip to be over and wishing that it would never end, that she and Cooper could drive forever towards the wide, empty horizon.

They got back to Bindaburra late that afternoon, having seen only a fraction of the property. The ute drew up by the veranda steps and Cooper switched off the engine. For a moment neither of them moved. The silence vibrated with tension until, inevitably, they both started to speak at once.

They broke off awkwardly. 'You first,' said Cooper.

Darcy wasn't even sure what she had been intending to say. She wanted to tell him what the trip had meant to her. He had given her memories to treasure, of the space and the light and the way she had felt sitting next to him high on top of the sand-dune. It wasn't his fault that the sights and the sounds and the smells of the creek should be inextricably associated with the hopelessness of loving him.

'I just wanted to say thank you,' she said lamely. 'It was a very... interesting... trip.' It sounded horribly inadequate even to her own ears.

Cooper's eyes were shuttered, unreadable. 'I'm glad you enjoyed it,' he said so formally that Darcy felt crushed.

'Well... I'd better go and do something about supper,' she said brightly, and got out. When she closed the door behind her, it felt as if she was closing off all hope.

The conversation over the meal was confined exclusively to the work the men had been doing in their absence and some animated reminiscences about breaking horses, neither of which left much for Darcy to say. She sat feeling miserable and out of place. Cooper had barely given her time to get out of the car before he had driven off to find the ringers, obviously desperate to get back to work, and now the conversation seemed expressly designed to underline the fact that she might climb a few sand-dunes and learn to admire a tree-lined creek, but she would never belong, and the sooner she accepted it the better.

Fiercely glad now that she hadn't had the courage to tell Cooper that she was in love with him, Darcy cleared up silently and then announced that she was tired and was going to bed.

They all murmured goodnight, but it was clear that their minds were still on branding calves and mending fences. Cooper only nodded and didn't look at her.

Resisting the urge to slam the door behind her, Darcy marched down the corridor to her room and slammed that door instead. She was *not* going to cry!

She scowled at her furious reflection in the mirror. What had possessed her to think that she was in love

with anyone as disagreeable as Cooper Anderson? She
was just a servant as far as he was concerned, there
to cook and to clean and to be placated by a token
drive around her own property! Darcy comforted
herself that she hadn't blurted out some stupid story
about being in love with him. She had spared herself
that humiliation at least.

She wasn't tired at all, but now she would have to
spend the rest of the evening in her room. The thought
didn't improve Darcy's temper. She had had a shower
before supper, so she couldn't even waste time doing
that.

For want of anything better to do, Darcy put on
the pale yellow pyjamas she had discovered in Uncle
Bill's drawer. Several washings had left them wonderfully soft, and although Darcy pretended she only
wore them out of necessity she secretly rather enjoyed
their old-fashioned comfort. Rolling up the legs and
sleeves and drawing the cord as tight as she could
round her slender frame, she padded across the corridor to the bathroom.

Unfortunately, washing her face and brushing her
teeth had only wasted five minutes. A long evening
stretched ahead until Darcy remembered the meagre
collection of books in the sitting-room. When she had
looked before they had seemed to be a very odd
mixture of airport paperbacks and dusty classics, but
there had to be something there that would take her
mind off Cooper.

She was halfway down the corridor when the
kitchen door opened and Cooper came out. Darcy
stopped in her tracks. In the dim light of the single
naked light bulb she looked very young and impossibly slender in the loose, lemon-coloured pyjamas.

Her eyes were dark and wary, her expression curiously vulnerable as she pushed her dark hair away from her face.

'I thought you were tired?' Cooper walked towards her, his face closed and hard.

'I am,' said Darcy. Her anger had evaporated and she felt ridiculously nervous. 'I was just going to get a book from the sitting-room.' Why was she explaining herself to him?

'So you're not too tired to read?'

The harshness in his voice brought a spark of defiance to Darcy's eyes. 'I thought it would be more entertaining than listening to you lot at dinner!' she said waspishly. 'I'm surprised you could drag yourself away from such a *fascinating* conversation!'

'I had to catch up on what had been going on while we were away,' said Cooper with a touch of irritation.

'What, all evening? Anyone would think we'd been away two weeks instead of two days!'

'A lot can happen in two days,' he pointed out coldly. 'I can't afford to waste time without making up for it afterwards.'

'I'm sorry my company was such a waste of time for you!' snapped Darcy, and he sighed.

'Don't be silly, Darcy,' he said, a tell-tale muscle hammering in his jaw. 'I've got to know what's going on, and if you had any interest in Bindaburra you'd want to know too. Instead of sulking all through dinner, you could have been listening and learning, but you couldn't do that, could you? You couldn't sit quietly and let others do the talking. You want everyone looking at *you*. I've just devoted two days to showing you round Bindaburra, but that's not enough for you, is it? You made everyone un-

comfortable by stalking off like that, and all because
for once we weren't paying you attention!'

'The last thing I want is for *you* to pay me attention!' flared Darcy, clenching her fists.

Cooper took a step nearer. 'Then what exactly is it
that you want, Darcy?'

'I don't want anything from you!' As he came
closer, she stepped back, but he reached out without
haste and took hold of her wrist, pulling her inexorably back towards him.

'Don't you?' he asked softly. His other hand cupped
her chin, and his thumb stroked the line of her jaw
almost thoughtfully. 'Are you sure?'

Darcy's eyes were huge and dark as she stared up
at him helplessly, awash with a terrible, shameful
longing. It wasn't fair, the way he could banish anger
and bitterness and resentment with a brush of his
fingers. One strong brown hand still circled her wrist,
but she knew that she could break free easily enough.

If she wanted to...

The light graze of his thumb was melting her bones,
shredding her resolution. Remember how angry you
were a minute ago, Darcy told herself desperately, but
she couldn't think beyond this moment, with the
harshness fading from Cooper's face and a new, much
more disturbing expression taking its place, an expression that made her heart slow until she could
hardly breathe.

'It isn't this that you want, is it?' he went on, his
voice very deep and low as he bent his head and
touched his lips to the sensitive place just below her
ear in a feather-light kiss.

Darcy caught her breath as desire prowled down
her back and dug its claws into the base of her spine.

'No,' she whispered, clinging to the last shreds of her pride.

The hand that had been caressing her face slid beneath the silky dark fall of hair to stroke the nape of her neck while he teased tiny kisses along her jaw. 'Is it this?' he breathed.

'N-no,' said Darcy, but so uncertainly that she could feel him smile against her cheek.

'No?' Releasing her wrist, Cooper's other hand drifted up her shoulder and then smoothed down her spine, feeling the way she quivered beneath his touch. 'This, then?' he murmured as his lips continued their leisurely progress towards her mouth.

They were almost, *almost* touching, were only a tantalising heartbeat away. Torn, tempted, tangled in longing, Darcy gave in.

She lifted her hands to his chest and spread them as if considering, a tiny smile tugging at the corners of her mouth. 'Maybe,' she said.

Cooper was smiling too, deliberately tormenting her by trailing kisses on past her mouth to explore her other cheek. 'You don't sound very sure,' he teased.

Darcy's hands moved up to his shoulders. It was too late to pretend. 'I am now,' she promised softly, and then the teasing was over as their lips sought each other and met at last.

It was a deep, hungry kiss, releasing the electric tension between them and infusing it with a new, shared urgency that swept all doubts and reservations away. Nothing mattered now but the blissful relief of being able to kiss at last, to be able to wind her arms around his neck and melt into the hard security of his body, to feel his lips and taste his mouth and let herself sink down into the intoxicating pleasure of his touch.

Breathless, they broke apart only to kiss again, mumbling each other's name, laughing shakily, neither prepared for the avalanche of emotion. Cooper's hands moved over her insistently, rucking up the pyjama jacket so that he could explore the smooth warmth of her skin, and, like a cat, she arched her back with a shudder of sensuous delight.

She never knew how long they stood there kissing beneath the naked electric bulb before Cooper drew her back down the corridor to his room. Darcy had never been inside it before, but she had no eyes for the masculinely uncluttered room or even for the big iron bedstead as Cooper closed the door and pressed her back against it, smoothing back her hair so that he could hold her face between hands that were a little unsteady.

'Darcy...' he said unevenly, kissing her eyes, her cheeks, her mouth again. 'Darcy, are you sure this is what you want?'

Her legs wouldn't have held her up on their own, and Darcy was glad of the door to lean against. Her face was flushed, her soft hair tumbling in disarray over his hands, and her midnight-blue eyes were dark and dilated with a desire that she was no longer afraid to reveal.

Her smile was slow and unshadowed. 'I'm sure,' she said softly, touching his cheek with a fleeting finger. 'I'm absolutely, completely, utterly sure.'

Cooper caught his breath and bent to kiss her again, a long, long kiss that was an unspoken promise of the joy that was to come.

She stood quite still as he slowly undid the buttons on the pyjama jacket and curved his hands around her breasts. His touch was fire against her skin, fire in her blood, scorching her senses and sending her spiralling down, down, down into a bottomless vortex of feeling. Dizzy, helpless, Darcy couldn't breathe, could only reach out for Cooper and cling to him, her one certainty when everything she had always held true was dissolving in this onslaught of sensation. She hadn't known that it was possible to feel this way, to be nothing but feeling.

Cooper was untying the cord at her waist, letting the baggy trousers whisper to the floor. His hands were more insistent now, his kisses more demanding, and Darcy was caught up in the irresistible rhythm of need. Fumbling in her haste, she unbuttoned his shirt, gasping with pleasure at the feeling of his bare skin touching hers at last. His chest was broad and muscular and unyielding, and she leant into him, glorying in his strength as he gathered her closer, repeating her name in a ragged voice that she hardly recognised.

Ensnarled in desire, Darcy reached for his belt, but her fingers were too clumsy, and in the end it was Cooper who undid it, dropping it to the floor where it landed with a clunk. The rest of his clothes followed swiftly, and then he was lifting her high in his arms and carrying her across to the old bed.

It creaked protestingly as he laid her down, but neither of them noticed. Stretching beside her, he let his eyes travel lingeringly over her slender body, luminous in the light of a single lamp, smiling at her sharp intake of breath as the long, strong brown fingers traced searing patterns of love over her satin-smooth skin.

'Do you know how long I've wanted to do this?' he asked huskily.

'How long?' she said with some difficulty, smiling, quivering beneath his touch.

'Since you waved me down beneath that ridiculous umbrella,' he told her, his hand still drifting possessively.

'I don't believe you,' she teased. 'You weren't at all pleased to see me!'

'All right,' he amended, 'since you came into that kitchen that evening with that defiant look in those big, beautiful eyes. Why do you think I was so bad-tempered?'

'Why do you think I was?' she countered softly.

Cooper leant over her, bracing himself on either side of her to look directly down into her face, and there was such warmth in his eyes that Darcy almost winced at the sharpness of the happiness that speared her heart.

'I thought you wanted Sebastian,' he reminded her.

'I didn't,' said Darcy, pulling him down on to her. 'I only wanted you.'

It was wonderful to be able to touch him at last. She ran her hands luxuriously over his back, feeling the texture of his skin and discovering the way his muscles flexed and rippled. His body was so strong, so compact, so balanced. Darcy wanted to discover every inch of him. She wanted to wrap herself around him and touch him and taste him and give him the same pleasure that he gave her.

His lips were at her throat, teasing along her collarbone, murmuring endearments into her breasts. 'I spent all last night staring up at the stars and thinking about how close you were,' he confessed. 'Thinking about this . . .'

Spreading Darcy's arms, he made her lie still as he kissed his way from palm to wrist, from the soft inside of her elbow to the pure curve of her shoulder and then enticingly down, savouring each curve and hollow of her body until she writhed in delicious torment and dug her fingers into his shoulders as she cried out his name.

'Please . . .' she gasped, inarticulate with longing. She was half frightened by the wave upon wave of uncontrollable sensation, and didn't know whether she was pleading with him to stop or begging him to go on.

Cooper smiled as he kissed his way back up from her toes to tangle his fingers in her hair, kissing her mouth almost fiercely. Released, Darcy wound herself round him frantically as the beat of passion grew ever-more impatient. Instinctively, they responded, moving together with increasing urgency and urged on by a pulse of excitement that threatened to overwhelm them.

Darcy clung to Cooper, awed by the glimpse of a feeling she had not even suspected existed. He was on her and within her and around her, and they were part of each other at last, and her eyes opened wide as he took her with him on a breathless plunge of excitement to the very threshold of ecstasy where they paused for one infinite, desperate moment before falling together through spinning delight to lie tangled and replete in each other's arms at last.

For a while there was only the sound of their ragged breathing as Cooper lay heavily on top of her, his face buried into her neck. Darcy's eyes shimmered with tears of incredulous happiness. Kissing his ear, she smoothed his hair tenderly, and he stirred and rolled on to his side without loosing his hold on her. Their breathing calmed gradually as they lay smiling into each other's eyes, exchanging soft, sweet kisses, nuzzling and murmuring lovers' words, exploring each other anew, but this time with slow, reminiscent caresses.

Later, Darcy rested her cheek against Cooper's broad shoulder and sighed contentedly. He held her into his side, warm and relaxed in sleep, and she listened to him breathing, feeling the steady rise and fall of his chest beneath her arm. Her fingers spread lovingly, smoothing over his flat stomach and drifting down his flank as she remembered the indescribable joy he had given her.

Darcy had never been so relaxed. She felt utterly peaceful, complete, somehow whole in a way that she had never known was missing before. She had no thought of the past or of what the future might hold. She had no thought at all. For now it was enough just to lie here beside Cooper and fall asleep to the slow, steady beat of his heart.

She woke to warm kisses and lazily drifting hands. 'This is your early morning alarm call,' murmured Cooper against her ear.

Darcy stretched voluptuously beneath his hands. 'It can't be time to get up already,' she protested sleepily even as her mouth curved in a smile at the tantalising trail of kisses being pressed down her throat.

'It isn't quite,' he confessed, raising himself on one elbow to smooth the dark, tousled hair tenderly away from her face. 'I just wanted to make sure that I wasn't dreaming last night.'

'If you were, I was having the same dream,' said Darcy, and pulled his head down for a long, sweet kiss.

'I had no idea you could be so nice at this time of the morning,' he teased her when he lifted his head at last. 'You must be getting used to the outback life.'

'That's because you never woke me like this before,' she said a little breathlessly. Arching responsively beneath his questing hands, she reached for him once more, and the cold, dark morning was forgotten as together they rediscovered the joy of the night.

When the alarm went off, Cooper disentangled himself reluctantly in spite of Darcy's mumbled protests and dressed swiftly. 'Come on, Cook. Up you get,' he said, retrieving her pyjamas from the floor and tossing them across to her.

'Can't we take a day off and stay in bed?' she grumbled sleepily.

'Where's your sense of responsibility?' Cooper pretended to be shocked as he helped her into her jacket as if she were a recalcitrant child. 'Think of those hungry men waiting for their breakfast,' he went on, doing up the buttons he had unfastened with such a tantalising lack of haste last night. 'Think of me,' he added, kissing her once, hard. 'And think of tonight.'

Darcy did think about it. She thought about nothing else as she washed dishes and swept floors and cooked meals in a glow of memory and anticipation that was rewarded when the men had left after supper and she and Cooper were alone at last.

It was the same every night after that. Darcy was bewitched by happiness, more aware, more *alive* than she had ever been before. She took pleasure in each tiny detail: the colour of the carrots as she peeled them, the crunching sound of the dried gum leaves underfoot as she walked down to the creek, the cool feel of the sheets as she made the bed. She felt as if a smudgy window had been cleaned, allowing her to see things in a sharp new light.

The routine didn't change. Darcy still prepared the meals and kept the house, but she sang as she worked, and the men appreciated the fact that her cooking improved dramatically, although she still had a tendency to drift off into a dream and burn the meat. She was still slow to get going in the morning, but it was doubtful if they would really have preferred her to be chirpy at breakfast. She was always sunny by smoko, and would sit and listen intently as they talked about the jobs that needed to be done on the property. She hadn't forgotten what Cooper had said to her that night. The ringers were suspicious at first, but when they saw that she genuinely wanted to learn what she could they would answer her questions patiently and gradually their barrier of reserve broke down until they were teasing her like brothers.

Cooper was out for most of the day, and Darcy treasured the time she spent alone with him. Most evenings when he came back dusty and tired they would sit on the veranda with a beer and talk as the sun sank over the creek in a blaze of colour. Leaning against him in the golden light, Darcy would tell herself that it was impossible to feel any happier—until the screen door banged shut behind the last ringer after supper, and Cooper turned to her with a smile and took her in his arms.

'Our month's truce is up tomorrow,' said Cooper one Sunday as they enjoyed the luxury of a lie-in until eight o'clock.

'A month? Is that all it's been?' Darcy lifted her head in surprise to look down into his face. Her dark hair swung forward and he tucked it carefully behind her ear, letting his fingers linger in its softness.

'It feels much longer, doesn't it?'

Darcy couldn't imagine a time without him now. A time when she hadn't known him, hadn't loved him seemed impossibly remote. 'We don't have to start fighting again, do we?'

He smiled as his other hand slid possessively over her slender curves. 'I'm sure we'll be able to renegotiate terms,' he said, and then his smile faded. 'If you want to stay, that is.'

Darcy looked down into his eyes, her own very soft and blue. 'I want to stay,' she said, and bent to kiss him.

Cooper's fingers tightened against her hair to keep her there, but there was no need, and his arms went round her as he swung her beneath him.

Much later, Darcy came back to earth with a sigh of sheer happiness. 'Wasn't the idea that I should be desperate to leave Bindaburra by now?' she murmured, her fingers playing lazily across his chest. 'I thought you were going to make things so unpleasant for me that I'd want to go home as soon as I could?'

'I changed my plan of campaign,' grinned Cooper. 'I could see that you were too stubborn to give in and then . . .'

'Then?' she prompted and he stroked her hair.

'Then I discovered that I didn't want you to go after all,' he said.

Darcy hugged his words to her all day. They had never spoken of marriage, and she was content for things to stay as they were for now. They had only

known each for a month, after all, and although
Cooper had never actually said that he loved her he
didn't need to. Sebastian had been all words, but
Cooper was all action, and he showed her how he
loved her every time he touched her. For now, that
was enough.

They were all sitting at lunch a couple of days later
when they heard a car draw up outside. Cooper went
out to see who it was, and came back a few minutes
later with a pleasant-looking couple and four children,
the youngest of whom couldn't have been more than
three or four.

These were the first strangers Darcy had seen in a
month, and it made her realise just how isolated
Bindaburra was. At home, she was the most sociable
of people, the life and soul of every party, and
although she hadn't missed her London life at all she
was delighted at the prospect of talking to someone
new.

She beamed a welcome as Cooper introduced the
couple as Carol and Peter Ridley. 'Sit down—I'll make
you a coffee.'

When she came back with the coffees, Cooper
looked down the table at her. 'Peter's just been telling
me that they've been bringing the children here for
three years now. Bill used to let them camp down by
one of the waterholes for a week.'

'That's right,' Jim put in surprisingly. He usually
only spoke when it was absolutely necessary. 'Mr
Meadows was happy to have them. He said they might
be city people, but they knew what they were doing
all right. They were always careful about fires, and
never left any mess behind them.'

Peter Ridley looked rather embarrassed by this un-expected tribute. 'We live in Adelaide, but we want the kids to learn to love this kind of country too,' he explained. 'We met Mr Meadows quite by accident one year, but he said we could camp here, and it was so beautiful that we haven't wanted to go anywhere else. We came here today to ask him if it would be all right for us to stay here again.' He paused. 'It was a real shock to hear that he was dead. He was a great guy.'

'Your husband was just saying that he thought it might be possible for us to camp again,' Carol Ridley added, making the obvious assumption.

'Only if you agree—partner!' Cooper put in suavely.

Darcy decided that it was too complicated to ex-plain that she and Cooper weren't in fact married. 'Of course,' she said. 'I'm sure Uncle Bill would want us to welcome you back.'

'It's very kind of you,' said Carol gratefully. 'We're quite self-sufficient, so we won't trouble you at all.'

Darcy was quite sorry to see them go. She had en-joyed talking to Carol, who was obviously puzzled by her, and had insisted on taking all the children to collect some eggs for them to take away. By the time they'd got back, they were all fast friends, and the children had had to be bundled into the car by their parents. They hung out of the windows as they drove away, waving back at Darcy.

'I see you've got some new fans,' said Cooper, coming up behind her and putting his arms around her. The ringers had disappeared back out to work and they were alone on the dusty veranda.

Darcy leant back comfortably against him, placing her hands over his at her waist. 'They seem like a nice family,' she said, unconsciously wistful. What would it be like to have children here at Bindaburra? *Their* children?

'It's good to see new faces every now and then,' said Cooper, misinterpreting her tiny sigh. 'I forget how bored you must be sometimes. You're not used to the isolation the way we are.'

'I'm not bored,' she said. 'I've been so happy I haven't needed anyone else but you.'

He kissed her neck. 'You still spend most of the day on your own. You need to meet more people.'

'What I *really* need to do is go shopping,' Darcy told him. 'I've let the stores run so low that I badly need to stock up. *Is* there a shop anywhere near here?'

'There isn't anything near Bindaburra,' said Cooper, amused. 'The nearest shop would be at Muroonda, but it doesn't have much stock. If you can wait a week or so, I'll fly you down to Adelaide and you can stock up on everything.'

'I think I'll need to get some basics before then,' she said, although the thought of having Cooper all to herself on a trip to the city was very tempting. 'How long does it take to drive to Muroonda?'

'An hour and a half, two hours, depending on the roads. We're a bit busy at the moment, though.'

'I can go by myself, can't I?' Jim and Gary had rescued her hire car from the mud soon after they'd returned, and since then it had been sitting outside the woolshed. 'I'm paying for the car, so I might as well use it.'

Cooper looked dubious. 'I don't like the idea of you driving around on your own. What if you get lost?'

'Then I'll stay in the car the way you told me to, and if I'm not back by dark you can come and look for me. It can't be that hard to find the way!'

It took some cajoling, but eventually Cooper agreed to let her go on her own. 'You're sure you know where you're going?' he asked as she threw her shopping-list on the front seat the next day.

Darcy waved the map he had drawn under his nose and kissed him goodbye. 'Don't fuss!' she said gaily. 'I'll be back before you!'

CHAPTER SEVEN

SPIRITS high, Darcy bowled back along the track towards the turn-off. Who would have thought she would ever be this excited about a trip to buy flour and sugar and a new dustpan and brush?

Muroonda was a wide, dusty street set down in the middle of nowhere, for no apparent reason as far as Darcy could see. At either end, the road stretched out to the horizon. According to the signpost, the nearest town in one direction was two hundred and sixteen kilometres, and in the other four hundred and seventy-six. There was a pub with a turned veranda, a clinic, a garage and a small, dark shop whose shelves were lined with an odd assortment of goods. Tinned fruit sat cheek by jowl with shaving foam, prunes next to canned meat, biscuits by suncream. There was a fridge cabinet and a freezer and, displayed between plastic chairs and a tiny selection of greeting cards, a display of fresh fruit and vegetables.

The chatty man behind the counter told her that the delivery truck had only arrived the previous day, and wouldn't be back for another two weeks, so she had timed her visit well. It wasn't long before he found out exactly who Darcy was and what she was doing there. There was only one other person in the shop at the time, a lean, good-looking man dressed in moleskin trousers and an immaculate stockman's hat. He looked up from the mail he had collected and listened unashamedly when he heard that Darcy was from Bindaburra.

'Jed Murray,' he introduced himself with a charming smile. 'So you're Bill Meadows' famous niece?'

Darcy found herself responding to his smile. He was certainly handsome, and had a certain sophisticated air that seemed oddly out of place in this cluttered shop. On closer inspection, she noticed that his boots were highly polished, his shirt tailored and his nails very clean, and she wondered what he was doing out here. He didn't work like Cooper, that was for sure!

Whatever he did, he knew how to charm. Before she quite knew what was happening, Darcy found herself completing her purchases and being steered along to the pub for a beer. 'Bill's niece deserves a proper welcome,' he insisted when she tried to demur.

Darcy allowed herself to be persuaded. After all, Cooper had been telling her she ought to meet other people and Jed Murray couldn't have been more friendly and welcoming. It sounded as if he had been a good friend to Uncle Bill, too, and she warmed to him at once, although nagged by a strange feeling that she had met him somewhere before.

'Cooper's obviously been keeping you to himself,' said Jed when they were settled with their drinks. 'Now I wonder why that is?'

'We've been very busy,' said Darcy, blushing slightly.

'Cooper always was very busy.' The comment, innocuous enough, held an undercurrent of sneering dislike and she glanced at him, puzzled, wondering why Jed should sound so resentful of Cooper. Seeing

her frown, Jed smiled so boyishly that she decided
she must have imagined it. 'We'll soon put that right,
though. It's my wife's birthday a week on Saturday
and we're having a bit of a barbecue at our place to
celebrate. It's not far from here and everyone will be
there, so it'll be the ideal opportunity to introduce
you. Why don't you come? And Cooper, of course,'
he added after an almost imperceptible pause.

'Well...' Darcy wasn't quite sure why she hesitated. Surely this was just what Cooper had meant?
Jed was charming and it was a very generous invitation to a stranger, even if he had been a friend of
Uncle Bill's. 'Thank you,' she said, making up her
mind. 'I'd love to come and I'm sure Cooper would
too.'

Cooper soon disabused her of any such idea. 'You
said *what*?' he shouted when Darcy told him of the
invitation.

'I said we'd both love to go,' repeated Darcy,
surprised.

'We would *not* love to go,' said Cooper tightly. He
got up from the seat and strode over to stand at the
veranda rail, looking out at the corellas screaming and
swooping over the creek.

Darcy looked at his rigid back in perplexity. 'Why
on earth not? I thought you wanted me to meet more
people?'

'I don't want you to meet people like Jed Murray!'

'But he was charming,' she protested.

Cooper swung round. 'Oh, he's charming all right!
Too charming.'

'That's ridiculous!' said Darcy, beginning to lose
her temper. The more she had thought about it on

the way home, the more she had looked forward to going to the barbecue with Cooper and being introduced to people as his future wife, as someone who belonged. Now he was spoiling everything! 'He seemed perfectly nice to me. In fact, he was more than nice. He was friendly and welcoming—which is more than you were when I first arrived, if you remember!—and I can't see any reason not to accept his generous invitation.'

'I don't trust him, that's why not,' said Cooper between clenched teeth.

'You can't just say you don't trust him without giving a reason!'

His eyes shuttered. 'My reasons are my business,' he said flatly.

'Great!' Darcy jumped up from the seat, angry and hurt at the way he had simply shut her out. She had thought they trusted each other more than that. 'It doesn't matter that *I* was looking forward to the party! Oh, no, I'm supposed to stay stuck at home until you decide you're ready to go out!'

'If you're so desperate to get away, you go,' said Cooper harshly.

'Right, I will!'

They glared at each other. 'I might have known that you'd fall for Jed's line,' he accused her, a muscle jumping in his cheek. 'You love that pseudo-smoothness and sophistication, don't you? I'll bet Sebastian was just the same.'

Now that he had said it, Darcy realised that Sebastian was exactly the person Jed had reminded her of, but she had no intention of admitting as much to Cooper.

'If I liked smoothness and sophistication, I would hardly be here with you, would I?' she said nastily. 'And I don't see how inviting me to his wife's party can be a *line*! Nor do I see why I should have to give up a chance to go out and meet new people just because you're too stupid and pigheaded to come with me!'

Whirling round, she stalked back into the kitchen, letting the screen door bang furiously back into place behind her. Her eyes were stormy and bright with tears that she was determined not to shed. She couldn't understand why Cooper was being so unreasonable, and she was hurt by his refusal to tell her why he disliked Jed so much. Surely they were close enough by now not to have secrets from each other?

The meal that night was tense and uncomfortable. At least, it was for Darcy. There was a grim set to Cooper's jaw, but otherwise he was quite expressionless, and managed to carry on an infuriatingly normal conversation with Gary about bull-roping until Darcy wanted to scream. How could he carry on as if nothing had happened? She was shocked and distressed by how suddenly the anger had flared between them, and if Cooper had had any decency he would have been too!

His apparent indifference only made Darcy even angrier, and when after supper he refused to discuss the matter any further she slammed out of the room and down to her old bedroom. It was the first time she had slept there since Cooper had taken her out to the waterhole, and it looked bleak and cheerless.

Darcy huddled under the sheets, cold and miserable and missing Cooper's firm body with a physical ache, but too proud to creep across the corridor to his room and slide into bed beside him. Why couldn't he come and apologise to *her*? She listened tensely for his footsteps, for his hand at the door, but there was only the sound of his door shutting firmly behind him and the click of his light.

The next day was hardly any better. He wished her a cool good morning and proceeded to discuss the day's jobs with Jim over breakfast. Effectively ignored, Darcy gritted her teeth and wondered why she had been stupid enough to lie awake all night wondering if Cooper was missing her as much as she was missing him. Obviously he hadn't! He looked as if he had had a perfectly good night's sleep, and now couldn't wait to get away from her again.

All the joy had drained from the day. The light was duller, the air less sharp. Even the parrots darting around the creek seemed less brightly coloured than usual, and the ceaseless 'aah-aah-aah' of the crows matched Darcy's mood perfectly.

Had it just been wishful thinking to imagine that Cooper loved her? Why *hadn't* he ever said that he did? The bleak suspicion that he might not after all crept into Darcy's heart and lodged there like a splinter of ice. She wished she had never gone to Muroonda, never met Jed Murray, never said that she would go to his wretched barbecue. She didn't want to go without Cooper. She didn't want to do anything without Cooper.

It was stupid to quarrel about something so trivial, she decided. So what if he didn't want to tell her about Jed? What did it matter compared to their happiness together? And why did she have to wait for him to say that he loved her? She could just as easily tell him first. There was no point in hanging on to pride when it only made her miserable. Darcy watched a pelican glide past without seeing it, filled with a new resolution. As soon as Cooper came back, she would tell him that he was far more important to her than any party.

She was waiting for him on the veranda as he came up the steps that evening. He was later than usual, and the sky was lit only by a red glow along the horizon.

Cooper stopped as Darcy stepped forward out of the shadows, and for a moment they looked at each other in silence. A rectangle of checkered light from the open door threw his face into harsh relief. He looked tired, Darcy thought with a wrench of her heart and a sudden leap of hope that perhaps he hadn't slept much last night after all.

'Hello,' he said carefully.

'Hello.' In spite of her resolution, Darcy felt stupidly, ridiculously shy. 'You're late tonight.'

'We've been mending fences,' he said. 'It's taken over an hour to get back, so the boys will be later too. Dinner will keep, won't it?'

Darcy nodded. This careful politeness was worse than fighting! How could she tell this cool, distant man that she loved him?

There was an awkward pause.

'Cooper——' she said, taking the plunge, but she never got any further. The sound of a car being driven fast across the cattle-grid made them both jerk round. It stopped unevenly and Carol Ridley stumbled out, followed by the two eldest children who were both crying.

Even in the darkness she looked ghastly, and Darcy ran down the steps behind Cooper. 'Carol! What is it?' she asked in concern, putting one arm round the distraught woman and the other around the children.

She was shaking so hard that she couldn't speak at first. 'It's Ben,' she managed at last.

'The little one?' Darcy felt herself go cold as she remembered the little boy who had held her hand so confidently as they'd walked down to collect the eggs. 'What's happened? Is he ill?'

Carol shook her head. 'He's lost...please, can you help? We've looked everywhere, but it's dark now and the batteries in our torch are going... Peter's still looking, but Ben's only four. I thought he was asleep in the tent... Oh, God, what if something's happened to him——?' She broke off as panic overwhelmed her once more.

Appalled, Darcy looked at Cooper, trusting instinctively that he would know what to do. He took Carol by the shoulders and turned her to face him. 'Listen, Carol, I'm going to get the men and some torches and we'll go and help Peter now, but you must stay calm and tell us exactly where he is first of all.'

Darcy watched Carol respond to the comforting strength of his hands and the infinitely reassuring steadiness of his voice. She pulled herself together with an effort and told him where they had been camping and he gave her a quick hug.

'Good girl. Now, I want you to stay with Darcy. I won't tell you not to worry, but the boys and I know that area better than anyone, and we'll find Ben for you as soon as we can. You'll look after them, won't you, Darcy?' he added over Carol's head, and Darcy nodded, the awkwardness between them quite forgotten in the face of this new crisis.

'Of course.'

Cooper disappeared at a run in the direction of the ringers' quarters and in an astonishingly short space of time two vehicles were heading at speed out of the gate.

The frightened and bewildered children were clinging to Darcy now, and she gave them a reassuring hug. 'They'll find Ben in no time,' she told them, but her heart was cold with fear for their brother. She remembered how easy it was to get completely lost, and if the outback had been an alien and menacing place in the broad daylight, how much worse would it be for a small child at night?

She kept her thoughts to herself, though. Carol was weeping quietly now, and Darcy wanted to get them all inside out of the cold. She made Carol a cup of strong, sweet tea and gave the children a piece of chocolate cake before gradually coaxing the whole story out of them.

Carol had put Ben to sleep in the tent while the older children played down by the creek. Peter had been gathering firewood, but Carol herself had stayed near the tent the whole time. 'I don't know how Ben could possibly have slipped out without me seeing him,' she said tearfully, clutching her hands around her mug. 'I remember I went down to the creek to sort out some squabble the children were having, but that was only yards away, and I couldn't have had my back turned for more than a couple of minutes.'

They hadn't discovered that Ben was gone until Carol had begun to wonder why he was sleeping so long and had gone to wake him up. Since then they had all shouted themselves hoarse, combing the area around their camp until it had begun to get dark and they had realised that they needed help. 'So I c-came

to you,' Carol finished. 'I know we said we wouldn't
be any trouble, but we didn't know what else to do.'

'You did exactly the right thing,' said Darcy firmly.

'Your husband was wonderful,' the other woman
said, wiping her eyes with a crumpled tissue. 'He
didn't say very much, but I knew he'd take charge of
everything. There's something *safe* about him. Do you
know what I mean?'

Darcy knew what she meant. Her face softened unconsciously. 'You know that nothing can go wrong as
long as he's there?'

'Yes, that's it exactly. I just hope...' Carol trailed
off, and her mouth wobbled as fears for her son
crowded in again.

Deciding that it would be easier for the frantic
woman if she and the children had something to do,
Darcy set them to making sandwiches and a Thermos
of coffee for the searchers. She hoped against hope
that they wouldn't be needed, but the men would be
hungry, she knew, and it seemed to be helping Carol.
Some colour had returned to her cheeks and the
children were brightening visibly, although by the time
everything was ready they were dropping with
exhaustion.

'I'll find you some sheets and you can put them to
bed here,' said Darcy with decision. 'While you're
doing that, I'll take the sandwiches down to the men
and bring you back the news as soon as I can.'

She hoped against hope that they would be heading
back to the house already, but the vehicles were still
ringed around the tent, and the first thing she saw as
she got out of the car was Peter Ridley's haggard face.
Darcy didn't even think about the fact that she hardly
knew him. Instead she went straight up and put her

arms around him in wordless comfort, and he clung to her with a sort of desperation.

'I know you won't feel like it, but you should try to eat something,' she said, and was pouring him a steaming mug of coffee when Cooper appeared. He was looking bleak, but his expression lightened when he saw Darcy with the coffee.

'Sensible girl,' he said, and in spite of the terrible situation Darcy felt herself glow at the warm approval in his eyes. He whistled for the men, who appeared out of the darkness one by one and fell on the sandwiches, shaking their heads helplessly as they reported their lack of success.

Unable to sit still while they took a well-deserved break and discussed how they would continue the search, Darcy picked up a torch and went down to the creek. Logically, she knew this area would have been searched first of all, but she made her way along the bank, flashing the torch into the undergrowth. Intent on her task, she didn't realise at first how far she had come until the flashlight caught the ominously familiar shapes looming through the darkness.

Darcy swallowed. She remembered these rocks only too well. Their eerie atmosphere had spooked her in the daylight, but by night the sense of the uncanny had deepened to menace, and she stopped, her heart hammering in her throat and her stomach churning with fear.

A four-year-old couldn't possibly have got this far, she reasoned. Anyway, the men would undoubtedly have been this way, and they obviously hadn't found any sign of Ben. The sensible thing would be to turn round and go back along the creek the way she had come.

But something drew her towards the rocks even as every instinct shrieked out in protest. 'Ben!' His name came out as a whisper as she set out across the sinister silence of the rocks, and she had to force herself to shout. 'Ben!'

Her voice echoed eerily and she shivered in spite of Cooper's warm jumper that she had pulled on before she'd come out. Her heart was knocking painfully and her hand was slippery around the flashlight. She had to keep stopping to wipe her palm on her trousers, terrified that she would drop her only light. The powerful beam intensified the smothering darkness which seemed alive with flickering, nameless fears.

Darcy never knew how she forced herself to the other side of the rocks, nor what made her shine the beam down between two boulders as she turned to retrace her steps. There, a small, pathetically white-faced figure lay huddled in an exhausted sleep.

It was Ben.

The relief was so great that for a moment Darcy couldn't move. All feeling seemed to drain out of her, only to return with such a whoosh that she felt light-headed. Somewhere in the distance, she could hear faint voices calling her name, but she didn't want to frighten the sleeping child by shouting.

Instead, she wrapped him in Cooper's jumper and lifted him in her arms. He wasn't light and she was hampered by having to try and keep the torch steady, but somehow she made it back across the rocks and began to head slowly along the creek-edge. She wasn't going to risk getting lost now.

'Darcy!' It was Cooper's voice, sharp with fear, but she still didn't dare cry out. It seemed like an age before she saw a flashlight swinging towards her, and when she saw it stop and steady on her she stood quite still, her legs trembling with exhaustion.

Cooper was running now. 'Darcy, what the hell do you think you're——?' He stopped abruptly as he saw what she held in her arms, and came quickly forward to relieve her of her burden. Ben lay so limp that he glanced at Darcy in concern. 'He's not . . . ?'

She shook her head. 'He's just exhausted,' she said, ashamed of the way her voice cracked.

'And so are you,' said Cooper roughly. 'Come on, let's get you both back to the homestead. You can tell us all about it when we get there.'

Darcy was so tired that she hardly took in the trip back to the homestead. She remembered Peter Ridley's face as Cooper handed him his sleeping son, though, and the desperate look in Carol's eyes as she came out on to the veranda to meet them. She knew that if she sat down she would simply fall asleep, so she forced herself to stay busy, making more tea and sandwiches for everyone and preparing a room for Carol and Peter. Ben was being kept warm, but didn't seem to have suffered more than cold and fright.

At last his parents, incoherent with gratitude, were persuaded to bed and the men disappeared back to their quarters. Darcy began gathering together dirty mugs until Cooper took them forcibly from her hands.

'You've done enough today,' he said, and held out his arms.

Darcy walked straight into them and rested her cheek thankfully against his shoulder, holding him tightly as his arms encircled her. 'You're a heroine,' he murmured into her hair. 'But don't you ever disappear like that again! When I looked round and saw that you'd gone . . .' His hold on her tightened almost painfully, but Darcy didn't care. 'I don't think I've ever been so frightened in my life.'

'I don't think I have either,' said Darcy, remembering the rocks with a shudder. 'I don't know what made me look there. It's such a weird place, and with all those cracks and crevasses it would have been so easy to walk right past him. It was sheer luck that I happened to look down just then.'

'If you hadn't been brave enough to look there, we might still have been searching.' Cooper put her away from him slightly so that he could look down into her face. 'When I wasn't scared stiff because I thought we'd lost you as well as Ben, I was very proud of you tonight, Darcy,' he said quietly. 'Carol said you were wonderfully calm and practical, and even the boys were impressed by the way you produced coffee and sandwiches with such a lack of fuss. You've done more than win their affection now, you've won their respect, and for a girl who can't even ride that's good going!'

'They must have thought I was pretty hopeless before if organising a few rounds of sandwiches was enough to impress them,' said Darcy a little wistfully.

'It was more than that. They say how you kept your head in a crisis, how you made yourself search even though you were terrified. They saw how cold and white and exhausted you were after carrying that child back.' Cooper paused. 'They saw what I saw, what none of us had seen before—that you could cope just as well out here as anyone else.'

Darcy felt as if he had just pinned a medal on her, and stupid tears stung her eyes. 'Do you really think so?'

'I do,' said Cooper gravely. 'I also think you are very tired. I know I am. It's been a long day, and for one reason or another I didn't sleep very well last night.'

'Nor did I,' she confessed.

'It was a stupid argument, wasn't it?' His arms tightened around her. 'I know I was unreasonable. I'm sorry.'

'I should have checked with you,' she said, rather muffled against his shoulder. 'I don't mind not going, really I don't.'

'Darcy——' Cooper broke off. 'Let's talk about this later. For now you need to get some sleep. You're exhausted.'

It was bliss to climb into the big iron bed again and slide down between the cool white sheets, to watch Cooper moving around the room with his deliberate, unhurried tread, smiling as he undressed. Half asleep as she was, Darcy's eyes lingered on the lean, taut body as he crossed to turn out the light, loving the clean, firm lines of him and the fluid ease with which he moved.

The bed sagged as Cooper got in beside her, and she turned towards him, sliding her hand across his chest and nuzzling into his throat. He sighed, a deep, contented sigh as his body relaxed, and Darcy snuggled closer. His arms went round her automatically and he kissed her hair, stroking one hand soothingly down her spine.

At least, he meant it to be soothing. Darcy found that it was having a very different effect. His body was so warm and solid next to hers, and, unbidden, desire uncoiled itself deep inside her, flickering tendrils along her senses. The slow, rhythmic stroke down her back was only making things worse.

Darcy's hand drifted lower.

'I thought you were asleep?' Cooper tried to sound stern, but Darcy could hear his smile. Encouraged, she wriggled up to kiss his jaw.

'I've woken up,' she whispered, kissing her way round to his mouth, her hair swinging softly over her face.

He tangled his fingers in it, holding her head down to prolong the kiss. 'You're supposed to be tired,' he reminded her, having ensured that she was thoroughly awake.

Darcy began teasing kisses down his chest, tasting his skin with her tongue, tantalising him with the silky tickle of her hair. 'I'm not tired any more,' she explained innocently, and smiled against his stomach as she inched lower. 'Are you?'

Cooper laughed and swung her beneath him. 'Not any more,' he said.

CHAPTER EIGHT

'WE CAN never thank you enough.' Peter Ridley wrung Cooper's hand while Darcy kissed the children goodbye. Ben didn't seem any the worse for his ordeal but they had decided to head back for Adelaide a couple of days earlier than planned just in case.

There were tears in Carol's eyes as she hugged first Cooper then Darcy. 'How will we ever be able to repay you? I wish we could give you something to show you how grateful we are, but I don't suppose they deliver flowers out here.'

Darcy laughed. 'I don't think they'd be in very good condition by the time they got here even if you could get someone to make the trip! Really, you don't need to thank us at all,' she went on more seriously. 'We're just glad Ben's all right.'

'I hope the experience hasn't put you off the outback for good,' Cooper added.

She had talked about 'we' and 'us', Cooper had stuck to 'I'. Did she sound too much as if she was trying to be the wife Peter and Carol so obviously thought her? In her relief at having made up that stupid quarrel, was she taking too much for granted? A tiny doubt crept into Darcy's mind as she stood beside him and waved the Ridleys off. Their love-making last night had been as glorious as ever, but Cooper had never even hinted at marriage. What if he was still waiting for her to sell Bindaburra?

Then Cooper turned to her and smiled, and all
doubts dissolved. 'I'd like to give you something too,
to thank you for last night, but, as Carol pointed out,
a dozen red roses are hard to find around here.'

'I'd settle for a night off from the cooking,' she
said lightly, spirits soaring at the look in his grey eyes.

'Done!' said Cooper promptly. 'How would you
like to sleep under the stars again?'

Darcy's eyes shone with eagerness. 'Could we?'

'If you promise not to wander off into the night
alone, the way you did last night!'

'I'll stick right beside you,' she promised.

It was late afternoon by the time Cooper stopped
the ute by a small waterhole overhung with ghost
gums, and the air was suffused with an unearthly
golden light. Cooper spread a rubber-backed rug on
the ground, and Darcy sat on it, leaning back against
the smooth trunk of a fallen tree and watching his
deft movements as he made tea in the battered,
blackened billy.

The corellas were as raucous as ever in the branches
above, settling in a ruffle of white only to explode
into activity again a few seconds later, but their din
was somehow part and parcel of the stillness and
silence settling slowly on the land. A few feet away,
the surface of the muddy brown water was reflecting
the intense blue of the sky, disturbed only by the occasional ripple of a jumping fish, and across the creek
the leaning gums were silhouetted against the setting
sun.

Darcy sat enveloped in the light. It glowed golden
on the curve of her cheek and the bloom of her skin,
gleaming in her dark hair and gilding the tiny hairs
on her arms. She felt utterly peaceful. A pair of the

pretty pink and grey galahs were sitting on a dead branch just above her and she raised a hand to shield her eyes from the glare so that she could see them better. Ignoring the corellas' racket, they preened each other, leaning together and rubbing their heads affectionately. They were so absorbed in each other that Darcy smiled.

Still smiling, she turned to point the galahs out to Cooper, only to find him watching her with such an intense expression that her smile faded. He had been about to pass her a mug of tea, but he put it back down on the ground.

'Will you marry me?' he asked, almost shakily.

Everything went very still and even the corellas fell silent. Totally unprepared, Darcy could only stare at Cooper, hunkered by the fire, the sun just catching the strong lines of his face. Had she heard him right?

'Darcy,' he said urgently. 'Say something!'

'Why?' she asked simply.

He made no move to touch her. 'Because I love you,' he said without taking his eyes from her face. 'Because I need you. Because I can't imagine life without you now.'

Darcy felt as if her heart had opened, sending an indescribably sweet warmth flooding through her. 'You've never told me that you love me before,' she said slowly, still trying to take it in.

'You must have known!'

'I thought you did,' she confessed, 'but I wasn't sure. Why didn't you tell me before?'

'Because I didn't know if you loved me.'

Neither of them had moved, but a smile trembled on Darcy's lips. 'You must have known,' she quoted his words back at him, and he did the same to her.

'I wasn't sure.'

'Well, I do.'

Cooper moved then. Crouching in front of her, he took her hands in his, and Darcy was inexpressibly moved to find that his weren't quite steady. 'You love me?' he asked as if he hadn't quite believed what she had said.

Darcy's eyes were soft and blue as she returned the pressure of his fingers. 'Yes.'

'Really?'

'Really,' she said gravely.

'Then you'll marry me?'

'Oh, yes,' said Darcy, and they both laughed at the wonderful, glorious delight of it. 'Oh, yes, I will!'

Kissing, still laughing, they sank down together on to the rug, giddy with the relief of loving and being loved, and then the laughter faded as they gave themselves up to the sweet rush of passion that drowned out all feeling other than desire.

The curls of dried bark dug into Darcy's back through the rug, but she didn't notice. Fumbling in their haste, they undressed each other, kissing and touching and kissing as they went, until at last there was nothing between them but the gasping thrill of skin on skin.

Darcy was molten beneath him, dissolved in the searing pleasure of his strong, sure hands on her body, arching at the touch of his mouth and the feel of his hardness. The light deepened from gold to orange to fiery red, sliding over the entwined figures on the rug as they explored each other with an almost fierce intensity, discovering new sensations, new joys, culminating at last in a cyclone of feeling that whirled them into the still centre of rapture and left Darcy sobbing Cooper's name as they plunged together into ecstasy.

Later, dressed once more against the cold, they sat together and watched the flames leap and flicker while the white gums loomed still and silent at the edge of the circle of firelight. Darcy leant back against Cooper's chest and felt his arms enclose her.

'When shall we get married?' he asked.

'Soon,' said Darcy. 'Only I'd like to tell my parents first.'

'Will they mind?'

'They'll mind not knowing you,' she admitted, and grimaced. 'I really ought to go home and reassure them that I'm not making a terrible mistake.'

'We'll both go,' said Cooper. 'Then I can reassure your father that I'll look after you properly.'

Darcy nestled back against him contentedly. 'He'll probably be delighted to hand on the job to someone else! He seems to have spent the last twenty-four years worrying about me. Are you sure you can spare the time to go all the way to England, though?'

'If you can wait a few weeks.'

'I can wait.' Darcy sighed happily. 'As long as I'm here with you.'

Cooper's arms tightened suddenly. 'Are you sure, Darcy?' he asked, suddenly urgent.

'About waiting?' She twisted round to look up at him, puzzled.

'About spending the rest of your life here,' he said. 'I know you've coped better than I ever believed possible, but it's only been a few weeks. You'll be a long way from your family and your friends, from your life as an actress, and there'll be times when the men and I have to be away mustering for days at a

time. Bindaburra can be a very lonely place on your
own, and in summer there are days on end when it's
too hot even to go outside.'

'You sound as if you're trying to put me off,' said
Darcy uncertainly.

'No, never that,' said Cooper quickly. 'I just want
to be sure that you've thought about what you're
doing and that you realise how hard life can be out
here at times. The weather's perfect at the moment.
The days are warm and sunny and the nights are cool,
and it's easy to forget what it's like when it's fifty
degrees and it's too hot to sleep.' He paused, searching
for the right words. 'I'll do everything I can to make
you happy, Darcy, but you need to know that there
are times when it's going to be hard.'

'That's true of any marriage, isn't it?'

'Of course.' Cooper stroked her cheek tenderly with
his finger. 'I'm not making a very good job of explaining, am I?'

'No, I do understand,' said Darcy. 'Or, at least, I
think I do. You want us to wait until I have a better
idea of just what life is going to be like.'

'I think it would be fairer to you,' he said. 'I don't
want to rush you into something you might regret,
that's all.'

'You know, my father is definitely going to approve of you,' said Darcy with a mock-sigh, a teasing
smile dancing in her eyes. 'You'll make a sensible
woman of me yet! I'll be lassoing cows next!'

Cooper laughed, but his hand tightened against her
face. 'Are you sure you don't mind?'

'Not as long as I can be with you,' she said, and
he kissed her.

'I'm beginning to think we should go to that party after all,' said Cooper, releasing her at last.

'I don't mind not going.' Safe here in his arms, Darcy didn't mind anything.

'No, you were right. You need to meet the other people who live out here. Besides,' he went on, 'I think it's time I met Jed Murray again—and his wife.'

Darcy sat up as a cold feeling trickled down her spine. 'His wife?'

'Melanie.' Cooper's voice was bitter, and she knew suddenly who had given him such a distrust of women.

'You were in love with her,' she said flatly.

Cooper took his arms away and leant forward to shift a log further on to the fire. 'We were going to be married.' His face was unreadable in the flickering light.

Darcy didn't want to hear about another woman Cooper had loved, but she couldn't help herself. 'What's she like?' she asked, trying desperately not to sound as jealous as she felt.

'She's very beautiful, very elusive.' He concentrated on the flames, as if remembering. 'Her father was manager of a smallish property in this area. He and his wife used to look at Melanie as if they could hardly believe they had produced such a delicate, ethereal creature. She was an only child, and they doted on her, treating her like a little princess who had to be shielded from the roughness of outback life. Melanie never rode or worked on the property. She used to read and dream instead.'

Cooper paused and poked the fire again. He didn't look at Darcy, who sat hugging her knees and watching his profile. 'Melanie was always different,' he went on after a moment. 'As a young girl, she had

a fey quality, a sort of mysterious innocence that was
very intriguing.' His mouth twisted. 'I used to think
that her aloofness made her special. Later I learnt
that it just meant that she was utterly self-centred.
Melanie's not interested in anyone other than herself.'

'She must have been interested in you if she agreed
to marry you,' said Darcy quietly.

'She was interested in what I represented,' said
Cooper. 'After my grandfather lost Bindaburra, my
father built up another property from scratch, and
we've prospered. Melanie saw the Anderson wealth
as her ticket out of here. Behind that quiet, innocent
front that we all found so mysterious she was relent-
lessly ambitious. She was determined that she was
going to be "somebody" and she was just biding her
time until her chance came. For a time I was that
chance, and then a better one came along.'

'Jed Murray?'

'Exactly. He was a slick city property dealer who'd
somehow managed to wangle himself an invitation to
come and stay with my parents. I was running one of
our other properties then, but I happened to take
Melanie there one weekend soon after we were engaged.' He glanced at Darcy. 'She left with Jed, and
I haven't seen her since.'

Darcy wasn't deceived by that flat, deliberately expressionless tone. The bitterness and humiliation
would have been hard for a man as proud as Cooper
to bear, and she felt anger burn along her veins. 'How
could she do that to you? How *could* she? Did she
say anything?'

'Oh, yes, it was quite a revelation,' said Cooper
drily. 'You have to understand what she was like. Just
getting her to notice me had been a challenge. It was

like trying to tame a wild animal, and I was too taken up with my pursuit to realise that I was the one being trapped. She was so delicate and fragile . . . I had no idea what she was really like until she announced that she was going to marry Jed. He'd promised her all she ever wanted, she said. She wanted to live in the city and enjoy herself, not be stuck out on a property. She wanted to be able to go shopping, to dress up and dine out at restaurants and give parties.' He shook his head. 'I had no idea that so much hatred boiled beneath her cool surface. It was as if she was transformed in front of my eyes. She had a chance to take what she wanted, and she didn't care who she had to hurt in order to get it.'

'I'm sorry,' said Darcy inadequately. 'It must have been awful for you.'

Cooper knocked some glowing coals off the log and sat back next to her, not quite touching her. 'I was shocked and humiliated, but mainly because I'd made a fool of myself. I couldn't believe that I'd never seen what she was really like, and I felt cold every time I thought about what it would have been like if I had married her. It was the luckiest escape of my life.'

'I wonder if that's what Uncle Bill felt?' Darcy murmured, thinking of the torn photograph of her great-uncle's long-lost sweetheart. He had mended Violet's picture, though, and kept her letters, as if he had decided that his first love would also be his last. Cooper had kept only the bitterness of disillusion.

Another thought occurred to her, and it was her turn to study the fire. 'Is that why you don't want to get married straight away? Because you think I might be like Melanie, wanting to go back to the city?'

She couldn't keep the hurt from her voice and Cooper took her chin in his hand, forcing her head round to face him. 'You're nothing like Melanie,' he said roughly. 'Nothing! You're warm and vibrant and *real*. I never knew what Melanie thought. When I looked in her eyes, I only ever saw my own reflection, but when I look in yours I see love and laughter and light. You show your emotions instead of hiding them away the way she did. I've never known anyone as generous with their emotions: your eyes flash when you're angry, but when you laugh you throw back your head and laugh properly, and when you love...' He dropped his voice as his thumb caressed her mouth. 'When you love, Darcy, you give all of yourself. Don't ever compare yourself to Melanie. What I felt for her was a boy's infatuation. I couldn't love her because I could never know her. What I feel for you is something quite, quite different. You must believe that.'

In the silence, a piece of wood spat and crackled on the fire. Darcy laid her palm against Cooper's cheek. 'I do,' she said, leaning forward to kiss him.

His arms came round her then, and he kissed her back fiercely. 'When I met you, it was as if I'd been waiting for you my whole life,' he told her. 'It didn't matter that you were the complete opposite of everything I'd told myself a good outback wife should be.'

'Now I understand why you were so angry when you heard I'd met Jed,' said Darcy, snuggling back against him with a sigh of happiness. 'Is that why you distrust him so much—because of what happened with Melanie?'

'It's one of the reasons. I was more jealous because you said you liked him so much. I know how at-

tractive he can be to women. He's charming, sophisticated, very persuasive. I was afraid he'd reminded
you of the kind of life you'd led in London, the kind
of life Melanie wanted so badly.'

Darcy frowned, puzzled. 'If she was so desperate
to get to the city, what are they doing up here having
a barbecue for her birthday? It sounded so homely
when Jed invited me!'

'A homely barbecue is one thing it won't be,' said
Cooper with a sudden grin. 'Oh, I dare say there'll
be some grilled meat on offer, but it'll be cooked by
chefs and served by waitresses. Melanie is apparently
into entertaining in the grand style.'

'Do you mean they live here now?'

'No, they've got a huge house in Adelaide where
Melanie spends as much time as she can. Ironically,
Jed has a real thing about the outback. He puts on
his boots and his hat at the first opportunity, but he
can hardly sit on a horse, and he certainly never gets
his hands dirty. He's a businessman who's made a
fortune out of oil, but he keeps a property up here
for show and likes to impress his city friends by flying
them all up for a weekend. If he's entertaining,
Melanie comes with him, but otherwise she never
comes near the place.'

'I don't think we should go,' said Darcy. 'It doesn't
sound as if I'd meet anyone local there anyway.'

'Oh, they'll all be there, invited for local "colour",
of course, but the food will be good and there'll be
plenty of free beer. No, let's go and show Melanie
what a big favour she did me by walking out all those
years ago!'

That night, Darcy lay in her bed-roll close to
Cooper's and thought about what he had told her.

She wished she had known about Melanie before. It explained so much of his initial suspicion of her. She must have seemed just the same, Darcy realised with a grimace, turning up in her smart city clothes to see what she could get out of Bindaburra. The miracle was that he had fallen in love with her at all.

Cooper loved her. Extravagant, impractical, unsuitable as she was, he loved her. Darcy shivered with happiness, and turned on her side so that she could study his face in the starlight. In sleep, the watchful expression relaxed, and he looked younger, less implacable. A wave of tenderness swept over Darcy, and she reached out a hand to touch his hair. Cooper. Her husband. She tasted the idea, rolling its possibilities around her mind, and suddenly she wished she hadn't accepted the need to delay the marriage. No hardship could persuade her that her future didn't lie with this quietly sleeping man. Marriage meant sharing the hard times as well as the magic. It meant that she would be able to lie next to him like this every night, and fall asleep knowing that he would still be there when she woke.

Rolling back on to her back with a smile, Darcy looked up at the stars. The last time she had slept beneath them, their cold brilliance had only emphasised their distance and the impossibility of loving Cooper. Now the stars seemed to belong to her, their glimmering light bright and near and somehow familiar, beckoning to her with the promise of happiness to come.

'If you were wondering what to give me for a secret engagement present, a new cooker would be ideal!' Darcy dropped down on to the veranda seat next to

Cooper and blew some stray hairs off her damp
forehead. Wrestling with the oven door every time she
wanted to baste the joint had left her red-faced and
sticky.

Cooper's eyes glinted with laughter. 'I think you've
been out here too long, Darcy! I never thought I'd
hear you long for something quite so practical!
Wouldn't you like something a little more romantic?'

'Yes,' she confessed. 'On the other hand, if I have
to spend the rest of my life cooking roast beef, an
unromantic cooker might be more useful!'

'You can have a new cooker anyway,' said Cooper,
putting his arm around her. 'In fact, you can have a
whole new kitchen.'

Darcy sat bolt upright, scandalised. 'And they call
me extravagant! Do you know how much a new
kitchen costs? And that's before you get anyone to
deliver it out here!'

'Why do you think Melanie wanted to marry me?'
he retorted, amused. 'Money isn't a problem, Darcy.
You can do what you like with the homestead. It needs
some attention, anyway.'

'What if people think *I'm* just marrying you for
your money?' said Darcy, subsiding back against him.

'You're forgetting that you're not exactly a pauper
yourself. You own half of Bindaburra.'

'It's not the same as having cash in hand, though,
is it? I don't even know how I'm going to pay for
that car I hired. I wrote and told them that I was
keeping it a bit longer, but my bill's going to be huge
unless I take it back soon.'

'We'll take it back next week,' said Cooper soothingly. 'And if you want money, I'll give you some.'

Darcy hesitated, frowning out at the creek. 'It doesn't seem right to take money from you somehow. Not when we're not married.'

'I can buy your share of Bindaburra from you if that makes you feel any better,' he suggested. 'It'll all belong to both of us eventually, anyway.'

'How much is it worth?'

When he told her, her jaw dropped. 'I had no idea it was worth that kind of money!'

'It might be worth more,' said Cooper. 'We'd need to get an independent valuation, but it would be around that figure.'

Darcy had never even dreamt of having so much money. Until now she had cheerfully existed on an actor's erratic income and an unusually sympathetic bank manager. It was the first time she had realised that marrying Cooper would mean the end of that precarious existence. Inheriting Bindaburra had never felt like money, but wouldn't it be better to do as Cooper suggested, and let him buy her out so that she didn't have to rely on him for handouts?

'Let's do that,' she said, and he turned to look at her in surprise.

'Are you sure?' he asked slowly, as if he had expected her to reject the idea out of hand. 'Perhaps you should think about it some more. It's your inheritance, after all, and it's not as if you need to decide immediately.'

But Darcy had never been a ditherer. When she made a decision, she did it completely, the way she did everything else. 'No, I've made up my mind,' she said, getting up to check on the potatoes. 'I'll sell you my half of Bindaburra.'

She began to look at the homestead with a new eye, as a housewife instead of a housekeeper. Cleaning was no longer a chore as she mentally redecorated every room, planning how she would transform it back into the gracious family home it had once been.

Fired with enthusiasm, Darcy decided to tackle the sitting-room first. A fresh coat of paint would be a start, and she could do that herself. She began by clearing out as much as possible. The gloomy pictures came off the walls, and the books had their dust blown off before being carried along to another room. The rest of the furniture Darcy planned to push into the middle of the room.

There was a writing desk in one corner, half hidden behind a winged chair. Darcy had never even noticed it before, and she opened it curiously.

Inside was the usual clutter of pens and pencils, a calendar that was five years out of date and a writing pad together with a motley assortment of envelopes. It looked as if this was where Uncle Bill had sat on the rare occasions when he had put pen to paper, and there were several letters crammed into the pigeon-holes.

Well, she might as well tidy it out while she was here. Darcy pulled out the letters and began glancing through them quickly to see if she could safely chuck them away, until a familiar letterhead caught her eye. She had received a similar letter from Uncle Bill's solicitors telling her about her bequest.

Her eye ran down the letter then stopped abruptly. Putting the other letters back on the desk, Darcy sat down very slowly on the spindly chair and began to read again.

Dear Bill,

Thank you for your recent letter, although I was
concerned to learn of your reservations about your
new partner. From what you have told me, there
seems little you can do to alter the contract at this
stage. You have not been in partnership long, and
it may be that matters will improve. However, if he
persists in his attempts to intimidate you into giving
up your share of Bindaburra, then I suggest that
you come and see me in Adelaide when we will be
able to judge what options are available to you.

As for your enquiry about leaving all your
property to your great-niece, I can, of course, draw
up a will to this effect, but inheriting a property
such as Bindaburra, especially under the condi-
tions you describe, would be a heavy responsibility
for a young girl with no experience of the outback.
You may want to consider other ways of expressing
your affection for her that might prove to be less
of a burden, but we can discuss this on your next
visit to Adelaide.

I am extremely sorry that you should be so distressed by your partner's attitude, but I trust that
matters will resolve themselves without recourse to
the law. If not, then you know that you may call
on me at any time, both as a solicitor and as an
old friend.

It was signed by the solicitor who had written to
her so kindly after Uncle Bill had died. Beneath the
cautious legal pomposity, Darcy recognised a real affection and concern for her great-uncle.

Very carefully, she laid the letter on the desk and stared blindly round the room as her blissfully happy dreams disintegrated.

There must have been some mistake, she told herself desperately. Surely Cooper couldn't have bullied and intimidated Uncle Bill in the way the letter suggested? Unbidden, a memory slid beneath her defences, a memory of Cooper looking at her with cold, implacable eyes. 'I want all of Bindaburra and I don't care what I have to do to get it.' Hadn't she herself accused him of trying to get rid of her? She had been convinced for a time that he was being deliberately hostile to try and persuade her to sell up and go. He had even admitted it.

Of course, that was before he had fallen in love with her, she reminded herself.

Or had he?

Was making love to her just another way to get what he had never made any secret of wanting—Bindaburra?

Darcy pressed her fingers to her temples, trying to deny the thoughts that came crowding in. Cooper smiling, Cooper reaching for her, Cooper oh, so casually suggesting that she sell him her share of Bindaburra so that she had some money of her own.

Had that been the plan all along?

'No!' Darcy stood up, hugging her arms around her as if to ward off the sudden cold. 'No, that's not how it was.'

Hating herself for her doubts, Darcy read the letter again. Only one fact was undeniable—that an old man had been distressed enough to write to his solicitors for advice. And Uncle Bill had not been a querulous old man who distressed easily. Darcy remembered him as a tough, indomitable figure, but it sounded as if he had been more than upset by Cooper's treatment. It sounded as if he had been frightened.

'It was a freak accident.' Wasn't that what Cooper had said about Uncle Bill's death? Had it been? Or had it been a little too convenient for him?

'Stop it! Stop it!' Darcy cried out loud. She shoved the letter back at the bottom of the pile and slammed the desk shut. She was being fanciful and reading things into the letter that weren't there. She loved Cooper; he loved her. He couldn't possibly have bullied Uncle Bill. It had all been some stupid misunderstanding that had blown over and left them the friends Cooper had said they had been.

Nothing had changed, she told herself desperately. But she knew that it had.

CHAPTER NINE

'ARE you sure you want to go?'

Cooper looked at Darcy with concern. She had been very quiet since the previous afternoon.

Darcy didn't want to go. It seemed a lifetime ago since they had sat under the stars and decided to face Jed and Melanie, utterly confident of their love for each other. That confidence was what she missed most of all. She still loved Cooper. Everything she knew about him told her that he had never treated Uncle Bill with anything but respect and affection, but that letter had been so *clear*. She couldn't rid herself of the image of her great-uncle sitting down to write a frightened letter to his friend, or forget the fact that in his distress he had been thinking of her. What would he feel if he knew that the niece he had entrusted Bindaburra to was gaily planning to hand it over to the very man who had tried to intimidate him into doing the same?

With all her heart Darcy wished that she had never read it, never opened the desk, never even thought about repainting the sitting-room. Now, no matter how she tried to convince herself that it had all been some misunderstanding, doubt had crept insidiously into her heart, and nothing would ever be the same again. Suddenly all Darcy's perceptions had shifted and darkened. Everything that had been so sure was now uncertain. It was as if a familiar landscape had changed without warning, its paths twisting into

151

sudden, treacherous dead-ends and the once solid
ground wavering beneath her feet.

Confused, despairing, torn between conflicting
loyalties, Darcy had fallen back on the clichéd excuse
of a headache, and had spent the night lying rigidly
on her own side of the bed. Now her head really was
aching and the last thing she wanted to do was drive
a hundred miles to a party. But she was afraid to be
alone with Cooper, afraid of blurting out her suspicions and seeing his face change.

'Of course I'm sure,' she said in a bright, artificial
voice, brushing her hair in front of the mirror with
intense concentration so that she didn't have to look
at him. 'I feel like a party.'

'It's just that you've been so quiet,' said Cooper.
In the mirror, Darcy could see him doing up the
buttons of a clean shirt. He had shaved, and his hair
was still damp from the shower as he regarded her
back with a slight frown. 'You're not sickening for
anything, are you?'

'I'm fine.'

'No bad news from home?' he persisted, unconvinced. Jim had brought the mail bag back from
Muroonda that afternoon, and there had been several
letters for Darcy from her family and friends, wanting
to know when she was coming home.

'No.'

Darcy stared at her reflection, wondering how she
could look so normal. Her hair still fell black and
silky to her shoulders, her skin was still smooth and
golden. Only the dull, desperate look deep in the dark
blue eyes gave any clue to the fact that inside her heart
was cracked and shrivelled. In an effort to make
herself feel better, she wore one of her favourite

outfits, a deep, rich red Indian cotton skirt with a dull gold thread running through it and an embroidered waistcoat. It made her look vibrant and colourful, almost gypsyish, but the sparkle that was so much part of her had vanished.

What would Cooper say if she turned round and told him the truth—that she was desperately afraid that he was not the man she thought he was? That she couldn't bear the thought that he might have frightened and bullied an old man? That she was realising that all she really knew of him was what he had chosen to tell her himself?

Darcy couldn't bring herself to ask him outright. She would have to find out the truth some other way, she had decided. Perhaps she could take the hire car back to Adelaide next week and go and see her uncle's solicitor? He would be able to tell her the whole story. He might even be able to tell her that she had got it all wrong, and then Cooper would never need to know about her terrible suspicions.

The thought of doing something practical cheered Darcy, and she turned from the mirror to toss a colourfully fringed shawl over her shoulders. 'I'm fine,' she told Cooper again. 'Let's go.'

Even so, she found it hard to behave normally, and it was a strained journey back towards Muroonda. Darcy kept her face averted, but she was very conscious of Cooper's searching glances. The darkness swallowed them up as the lights of Bindaburra disappeared behind the creek, isolating them together in the ute. The silence was agonising. Darcy tried to fill it with brittle chatter, but the words kept drying up and clogging in her throat, and Cooper refused to follow her lead.

'Why won't you tell me what's wrong?' he asked quietly as Darcy was racking her brains for some other subject to keep his inevitable questions at bay.

'Nothing's wrong,' she said, passionately grateful for the darkness that hid the tears stinging her eyes.

'You mean you don't want to tell me?'

'Nothing's wrong,' Darcy repeated stubbornly, and he sighed.

'All right, we'll leave it. Just let me know when you want to go home.'

If only she could. She longed to go back to Bindaburra, back to the time before she had found that letter, to a time when she had trusted absolutely in his love for her.

By the time they arrived, the party was in full swing. Cooper had been right in predicting that it would be no casual gathering of friends around a barbecue in the back yard. They parked in a paddock full of four-wheel drives, and on the other side of the track more small planes than Darcy had ever seen together before were ranged in lines by the airstrip.

There *was* a barbecue. In fact, there were several, attended by a team of trendy chefs in striped aprons, but this was evidently not a party where guests wandered inside to help themselves to a beer from the fridge or a cask of red wine perched on the edge of the kitchen table. Instead, pretty waitresses circulated round a huge marquee that was packed with an uneasy combination of chattering sophisticates and dour-faced farmers who stood around at the edge looking as if they would have preferred their beer out of a can.

Jed Murray stood at the entrance welcoming guests. He greeted Darcy with the smile that she remembered, as if out of all these people she was the one he had been waiting for. Except perhaps it wasn't quite as charming as she had thought. Now that she knew how he had run off with Cooper's fiancée, Darcy discerned a calculating look in his eyes. Then she remembered miserably that she had come to doubt Cooper's word about Uncle Bill. Should she not equally distrust his word about everything else?

Pushing the thought aside, she was in time to see Jed's smile freeze as he spotted Cooper behind her.

'Cooper.' He nodded but didn't offer to shake hands. 'I wasn't expecting to see you.'

'I heard that I was invited,' said Cooper, his eyes very cold. The antagonism between the two men was tangible. Darcy thought that they were like two dogs circling each other with their hackles up.

Jed had recovered his smile, but there was no warmth in it. 'Of course. I dare say you'll know a lot of the people here, and you'll want to catch up with Melanie, won't you? It must be years since you've seen each other.' The thinly veiled dislike in his voice made Darcy catch her breath, but Cooper seemed unperturbed.

'I'm sure she'll have plenty of other people to talk to,' he said coolly.

'Oh, but she'll want to make time for *you*. After all, you two used to be so close, didn't you?'

Darcy was beginning to wish they hadn't come after all. Sitting at home in silence would have been better than watching the sneer on Jed Murray's face and sensing the menace that shivered through the air. How could she ever have thought he was charming?

'You needn't bother dropping hints.' Cooper's voice was edged with steel. 'Darcy knows exactly how close Melanie and I used to be.'

Jed had clearly not been expecting that. 'So do we take it that this appearance of yours means that you're prepared to let bygones be bygones?'

'No,' said Cooper. 'It means that Darcy wanted to meet some new people and I didn't want her driving through the dark on her own.'

'Then she must meet Melanie first of all, mustn't she? I'm sure the two of them will have a lot in common,' said Jed maliciously. 'Darling!' He beckoned over Darcy's shoulder, and she turned to see Melanie waft over towards them.

She was just as beautiful as Cooper had said, with pale blonde hair the colour of rich cream and huge green eyes. Darcy looked at that angelic face and felt her heart contract. It was easy to see why Cooper had fallen in love with her. She was so tiny, so fragile, so exquisite that she didn't seem quite real. An air of incongruous other-worldliness hung about her. Darcy couldn't imagine Melanie ever washing dishes or peeling potatoes. She even seemed to float rather than walk, and when she faltered at the sight of Cooper standing by her husband Darcy thought that her shock was the only indication of her humanity at all.

Darcy glanced at Cooper, steeling herself to see the yearning in his eyes, but he was quite expressionless as he watched Melanie's approach. The four of them seemed enclosed in a tense bubble of silence quite apart from the noisy crowd around them in the marquee.

'Hello, Cooper,' said Melanie in a surprisingly husky voice.

'Melanie.' Cooper sounded cool, almost bored.

'This is Darcy Meadows,' Jed put in hurriedly. 'You remember I told you about the lovely girl I met in Muroonda?' he went on, putting a familiar arm around Darcy's waist. It was a gesture such as any host might make when introducing a new guest, but when Jed looked at Cooper he encountered a look that made him drop his hand with a falsely hearty laugh.

Melanie saw the look too, and the green eyes narrowed slightly. 'Of course I remember,' she said, a chill edge to the smoky voice. 'Jed was quite smitten, weren't you, darling?'

Cooper's jaw tightened, and Darcy rushed into the hostile silence. 'Er... happy birthday!'

'Why, thank you.' Melanie turned her enormous eyes on Darcy as if noticing her for the first time. Darcy was slender herself, but next to the other woman she felt huge and lumpy, and garish in her bright gypsy outfit. 'I'm glad you came.' She directed a sideways glance under those impossible lashes at Cooper. 'Very glad.'

Darcy didn't like the way Melanie looked at Cooper. It was a cool, speculative look as if she was wondering whether she could make him love her again, the way he had loved her before. 'I was expecting to stand around outside,' she said quickly, showing them the shawl draped over her arm. 'But it looks as if I'm going to be too hot. Is there anywhere I could leave this?'

She had hoped that it would be a cue for Melanie and Jed to move on to other new arrivals, but she had reckoned without Melanie.

'I'll show you,' she said and waved a languid hand at Cooper who had stepped forward. 'No, you stay here, Cooper. I'm sure Darcy will be able to find you again.'

Darcy had no choice but to go with her. Melanie led her across an immaculately mown lawn into the house, which looked as if it had been taken straight from the pages of an interior design magazine and dropped down here in the middle of the outback.

'What a lovely house,' Darcy murmured politely, privately considering it hideous. Design like this might be all very well in a city, but out here it struck her as bizarre, if not downright grotesque.

'It's not like Bindaburra, is it?'

'No, indeed,' said Darcy, glad to be able to agree whole-heartedly. Bindaburra might be a little dusty and neglected, but it had a quiet, understated elegance and a sense of belonging in its surroundings that this house would never have. 'You know Bindaburra, do you?' she asked casually, dropping her shawl on to a bed.

Melanie gave a humourless laugh, and for the first time Darcy noticed tiny lines of discontent around her mouth. 'How do you think I met Cooper?'

'I thought you grew up in the same area,' said Darcy uncertainly.

'Oh, we did. My father was your uncle's partner at Bindaburra.'

Darcy stopped dead. 'Your *father*?' she echoed incredulously, and Melanie's perfect brows lifted in surprise.

'Funny Cooper didn't mention it,' she said lightly.

Darcy didn't think it was funny at all. Her first reaction had been a leap of hope. She hadn't known

her great-uncle had had any other partners; perhaps
Melanie's father had been the partner Uncle Bill had
distrusted? But if that was the case, why had he given
up his interest to Cooper? And why hadn't Cooper
told her about it?

'Yes,' she muttered. 'Very funny.'

'Tell me,' Melanie went on, 'has Cooper asked you
to marry him yet?'

'I beg your pardon?' said Darcy stiffly.

'Oh, don't worry, he will!'

Darcy felt something cold close around her heart.
'I don't know what you mean. How can you possibly
know something like that?'

'Because I know Cooper,' said Melanie, her eyes
suddenly very green and cat-like. 'You forget that I
knew him a long time before you did. I was even going
to marry him. Did he tell you that?'

'Yes, he did. He also told me how you ran off with
Jed instead.' Darcy was proud of how steady her voice
sounded.

'Is that what he says?' Melanie smiled pityingly. 'It
doesn't sound to me as if Cooper has been quite honest
with you, Darcy. It was Cooper who broke off our
engagement, not me, and do you know why he did
that?' Darcy shook her head dumbly. 'Because he
discovered that my father had already sold his share
of Bindaburra. That was all Cooper ever wanted:
Bindaburra, Bindaburra... I was sick of hearing about
it! I was very young when we got engaged, and oh,
so naïve! Do you know, I really thought he loved me?'
Melanie shook her head as if in wonderment at her
own credulity. 'I soon learnt that all he really loved
was the idea of owning Bindaburra, and he was even
prepared to marry me if he thought that it would get

him Dad's share as a wedding-present. When he found
out that Dad had already sold it to Jed, that was the
end of our engagement!'

Darcy was beginning to feel sick. 'So you turned
round and married Jed instead?'

'You have to remember how young I was,' said
Melanie, ignoring her politely disbelieving tone. 'I
married Jed on the rebound, I admit it. I haven't re-
gretted it. Jed's been very good to me, but I don't
think I've ever quite gotten over Cooper. He's a very
special man, and when he's not obsessed with that
wretched property he can be quite charming and
dangerously   attractive...as   I'm   sure   you've
discovered.'

Darcy winced as a series of images spun through
her mind: Cooper brushing off his hat at the screen
door, his grey eyes warm and smiling; Cooper pulling
off his shirt last thing at night; Cooper sliding into
bed beside her, reaching for her... Involuntarily she
closed her eyes.

'He's been very...nice...to me.'

'I'll bet!' said Melanie, the everyday phrase sitting
oddly with her ethereal beauty. 'He must have hardly
believed his luck when he found out that Bill Meadows
had left everything to a single girl! It's not as if you're
unattractive either. I'm sure Cooper won't mind marrying you at all if he can't get Bindaburra any other
way, but I'd insist on a pre-nuptial contract if I were
you. Otherwise you might find life getting more and
more difficult until you're glad to let him have
Bindaburra if it means you can leave.'

'What makes you think there's any question of me
marrying Cooper?' asked Darcy, digging her finger-
nails into her palms.

'Oh, come on, it's obvious you're in love with him,' said Melanie with a patronising look. 'I'm just giving you the benefit of my experience, that's all. I wouldn't like to see anyone else hurt the way I was.'

Was that what she had been doing, passing on a kindly word of advice? Or had she been making trouble? Frowning, Darcy watched Melanie disappear back into the marquee. She hadn't liked Melanie and she hadn't trusted her, but her story had been sickeningly familiar, familiar enough to make Darcy wonder who was telling the truth. If it hadn't been for that letter, Darcy would have believed Cooper implicitly. As it was, she felt tired and confused and bitter at the growing suspicion that he might have been using her all along.

Coming out to Australia had been a terrible mistake. Hadn't her mother always told her that you never got anywhere by running away from your problems? She should have stayed in London where she belonged. Other actors were involved in flops or lost their boyfriends, but they didn't just give up and run off to the other side of the world.

Suddenly Darcy longed to be home with people she understood. Her heart wrenched at the thought of leaving Cooper, but she couldn't live with this terrible doubt. She would never be able to be sure of him again. When they got back to Bindaburra tonight, she would tell him some story about wanting to go home. She still had the car; she could leave tomorrow, and start trying to put this all behind her. Somehow, she would have to pretend that what she felt for Cooper was just an infatuation, as it had been for Sebastian.

A band had started up in the marquee, and a gabble of noise and laughter spilled out into the chill night

air. The sky was clear and already spangled with stars.
Darcy looked up at them, hugging herself against the
cold, and remembered another night like this when
there had been no marquee, no band, no smiling
waitresses or chattering crowds, only a still, silent
creek and Cooper's face in the firelight.

The memory brought a pain so great that Darcy
hunched herself as if against a blow and had to grit
her teeth to hold back the tears. The laughter from
the marquee seemed to mock her misery. Never had
she felt less like partying, but she knew that she would
have to go in there and pretend that nothing was
wrong. The prospect appalled her, but she wasn't an
actress for nothing—and indeed no one who saw her
laughing or dancing or chatting vivaciously that night
ever guessed that her heart was breaking.

Later, Darcy thought that it must have been the
best performance of her career. Never had she been
so witty, so entertaining, never had she flirted quite
so outrageously, gravitating instinctively to the social
set who had flown up from the city, and making sure
that Cooper could see just what a good time she was
having.

Not that he seemed to care. Darcy could see him
out of the corner of her eye, usually surrounded by
a bevy of socialites who were obviously smitten by his
lean body and air of quiet, controlled strength. Even
among this varied crowd he stood out. It wasn't his
height, or the way he was dressed. There were plenty
of tall, rangy men who looked as if they had just
swung themselves off horses. It was more to do with
the cool, contained way he stood, the way he bent his
head to listen to his companions, that compact, focused quality that was so distinctive.

Once while dancing Darcy saw Melanie shimmer up to him and lay her hand on his arm. To her intense frustration, Darcy's partner chose that moment to swing her round enthusiastically, and she only managed to manoeuvre back to an uninterrupted view in time to see Cooper say something to Melanie. His face didn't change, and he looked as pleasant as ever, but Melanie stepped back as if he had struck her.

What was the truth of the relationship between Cooper and Melanie? Darcy longed for Cooper to come and reassure her, but he seemed content to let her be monopolised by other men. He hadn't looked her way once, she realised miserably. If he had dragged her away, if he had kissed her and *forced* her to believe him, she might have changed her mind, but his lack of interest only strengthened Darcy's resolve to go. It obviously didn't matter to him one way or another as long as he got Bindaburra.

Darcy's jaw was beginning to feel rigid with smiling when Cooper finally materialised by her side and calmly handed her her shawl. 'It's time to go.'

'But I'm enjoying myself!' she lied. The group around Darcy added their voices to her protest, but Cooper ignored them.

'I don't care if you are or not, you're coming with me,' he said, and made sure she did by the simple expedient of taking her wrist in an iron grip and dragging her out of the marquee.

Once outside, he released her and strode on towards the ute, while Darcy followed sullenly, rubbing her wrist. The glittering, artificial air had dropped from her like a mask as soon as they'd hit the cold night air and she sat beside him in miserable silence on the long drive back towards Bindaburra, hugging her shawl around her for comfort.

They had just turned off the main track when Cooper stopped the car without warning and switched off the engine.

'What are you doing?' asked Darcy nervously.

'I'm not going any further until you tell me what's wrong,' he said. 'And don't bother telling me that nothing's the matter, because something obviously is. What did Melanie say to you?'

'Nothing that concerned you.'

'Come on, Darcy. You were gone for ages together. What did you talk about all that time?'

Darcy clasped her hands together in her lap. His hard voice was making her tremble with a mixture of anger and longing. 'If you must know, we talked about interior design,' she improvised desperately and unconvincingly.

'I don't believe you,' said Cooper flatly. 'A chat about decorating wouldn't make you behave the way you did tonight.'

'What do you mean?'

'You know perfectly well what I mean, Darcy.' He had turned in his seat to face her, his mouth set in a grim line. 'You deliberately avoided me all evening.'

'I didn't think you noticed!' said Darcy waspishly. 'Every time I looked round you were surrounded by women, and you weren't exactly beating them off!'

'*I* was trying to behave normally,' he said in a caustic tone. 'I wasn't showing off and throwing myself at every man I came across, which is what you were doing!'

There was a moment of taut silence, and then Cooper's face changed as he reached across and put his hand over both of hers. 'What is it, Darcy?' he asked more gently. 'You've been acting oddly ever since yesterday afternoon. Is it some news from home that's upset you?'

'All right, yes.' Darcy took a deep breath. 'It wasn't bad news, though. I...I had a letter from my agent. Apparently they're going to be holding auditions for a star role that she thinks would be ideal for me,' she went on, inventing desperately. 'She wants me to go home as soon as possible.'

Cooper took his hand away very slowly. 'And you're going to go?'

She nodded miserably, unable to look at him. Her hands felt very cold.

'What about us?' he said, not even bothering to disguise his bitterness. 'Have you just been amusing yourself these last few weeks? Is that it? I thought you loved me!'

'And I thought you loved *me*!' Darcy swung round, too hurt and angry to keep quiet any longer. She wasn't going to let him believe that it was all her fault! 'But you don't, do you? All you love is bloody Bindaburra!'

Cooper's jaw worked convulsively, but when he spoke his voice was as cold and as hard as steel. 'So you *have* been talking to Melanie. I might have known! What exactly did she tell you?'

'That you only wanted to marry her because of Bindaburra,' said Darcy, defiant. 'She said you were the one who broke off your engagement when you discovered that her father had sold his share to Jed.'

'And you believed her, I suppose?' said Cooper tightly. 'You'd met Melanie for five minutes, but you accepted everything she said without question! Do you

really believe that I would go to the lengths of marrying someone I didn't love just for the sake of a
property I could as easily buy?' He turned away in
disgust. 'There's trust for you! I thought the last few
weeks had meant more to you than that!'

'You're a fine one to talk about trust!' Darcy was
struggling not to cry. 'After the way you behaved to
Uncle Bill, I'm surprised you even know the meaning
of the word!'

Cooper went very still. 'What are you talking
about?' he said, dangerously quiet.

'You tried to intimidate him into selling his share
of Bindaburra to you, but it didn't work, did it? He
knew just what you were doing, and he decided to
leave it to me instead!'

'Did Melanie tell you that as well?' Cooper asked
sarcastically, and Darcy lifted her chin. She had gone
too far to back out now.

'No, she didn't.' Darcy drew a steadying breath. 'I
found a letter. Uncle Bill had written to his solicitor
because he was frightened of what you might do to
force him away from Bindaburra.'

'*Frightened* of me?' There was no mistaking the
shock in Cooper's expression. 'Is that what he said?'

'Not in so many words, but it was clear that he was
very distressed by what you were doing.'

There was another long silence. 'So you really think
I'm capable of bullying an old man off the property
he's loved for over forty years?'

Cooper's voice made Darcy flinch and she pressed
her hands against her eyes in sudden desperation. 'I
don't know what to think any more! I just want to
go home.' She couldn't fight the tears any longer. They

choked her throat and trickled down her cheeks, and she brushed them away angrily.

'Oh, I believe *that*!' said Cooper contemptuously. 'That's what this is really all about it, isn't it? It's nothing to do with Bindaburra and everything to do with the fact that you've decided you're bored and want to go home. The novelty's rubbed off and that grotesquely pretentious display tonight just reminded you what you've been missing! You should do very well in your audition, Darcy,' he added scathingly. 'You've had enough practice acting over the last few weeks, haven't you? And you're good, I'll give you that. I was so taken in, I didn't even realise it was all entertainment as far as you were concerned!'

'That's not true,' Darcy wept. 'You know it's not.'

'Do I?' Cooper's face was tight and closed. 'What about Bindaburra? Have you had enough of that too?'

'You have it if it means so much to you! I just don't care any more. I've already said I'll sell you my share, and I'd hate you to have to pretend to love me any longer than necessary!'

'I see,' said Cooper. 'Are you sure that's what you really want?'

'Yes,' she sobbed, beyond knowing *what* she wanted.

He switched on the engine and shoved the car back into gear. 'In that case, there doesn't seem anything more to say. I suggest you contact your solicitors about the sale as soon as you get home. Oh, and I'd insist on an independent valuation if I were you. Anyone who could bully an old man wouldn't think twice about cheating you over the price, would they?'

Darcy couldn't believe that he wasn't even going to make a show of trying to persuade her to stay. In spite of everything, it wasn't until then that she really believed that he didn't love her after all. It looked as if Melanie had been right. Cooper had got what he wanted—Bindaburra—and now he couldn't wait to get rid of her.

CHAPTER TEN

'IF YOU'RE driving down to Adelaide tomorrow, you'd better sleep in,' said Cooper, holding open the screen door with mock-courtesy. 'We wouldn't want you tired before you get to your audition, would we?'

Darcy wanted to weep again at his tone. 'What about breakfast?'

'We'll get it ourselves,' he said indifferently. 'I'm sure we'll be able to manage without you. After all, it's not as if we've never done it before. We'll be gone long before you're up.'

'Does that mean I won't see you again?' The words were wrung out of Darcy, and he turned with his hand on his bedroom door.

'I thought that was what you wanted,' he said, and went in, closing the door and shutting her finally out of his life.

Darcy stood quite still. She was utterly cold, and afraid that if she moved she would simply shatter into a thousand pieces of icy pain. Her mind refused to accept that she had seen Cooper for the last time.

She wanted to bang on his door, to burrow into his arms and let him persuade her that it had all been a horrible mistake. She wanted to fall asleep beside him and wake to normality. Tomorrow she wanted to bake rock cakes and clean the kitchen windows and sweep the dust off the veranda.

Instead she would have to get into a car and drive away from Bindaburra forever.

There was no one around when Darcy woke the next day, and the kitchen felt empty and echoing. Moving stiffly, she cleared up the debris from breakfast and left lunch ready in the fridge. When there were no more jobs she could do, she ran her hand along the edge of the old cooker and looked around her for the last time.

Then she walked slowly down the corridor to her room and picked up her bags. She had been careful to clear her clutter of cosmetics from the bathroom, and remove any of her clothes that had been so joyfully discarded in Cooper's room. When he came back, it would be as if she had never been here at all.

Darcy carried her bags out on to the veranda. It was another lovely day. A light breeze shivered across the surface of the creek, and the sun caught the brilliant white wings of the corellas as they flashed between the gums. A pelican was grunting for its mate on the far side of the water.

The creek would still be here when she was in London, Darcy realised. Nothing at Bindaburra would change without her. The corellas would still squabble, the trees would still lean over the water to admire their own reflections, the dust would still gather on the veranda.

Only she wouldn't be here. Panic gripped her mouth as she realised just what that meant. She would never sit here and watch the sunset with Cooper again. She would never hear the rooks complaining to each other, never walk down to the creek and breathe in the sharp, dry scent of the gum leaves underfoot. She would never be able to taste Cooper's mouth, touch his hard brown body, feel his hands drift warm and sure over her skin, would never again see his slow smile as he reached for her.

Never again.

The tears trickled unheeded down Darcy's cheeks as she walked down the veranda steps for the last time and put her bags in the car. Then she got in herself and drove across the cattle-grid and out along the dusty track without looking back.

The tracks had been graded since the rain and it was a much easier trip than before, but it still took Darcy nearly two days to get back to Adelaide. She spent the night at a motel in Port Augusta, but later the only thing she could remember was waking from a dream of Bindaburra to the desolation of a strange ceiling and an empty bed.

Adelaide was damp and grey, but she managed to get on a flight to Singapore the next day. As the plane accelerated along the runway, she wanted to shout at the pilot to stop and let her off, but it bore her inexorably aloft and further away from Cooper than ever. After that it was a blur of announcements and plastic trays of plastic food. Darcy put on her headphones so that she wouldn't have to talk, but her neighbour, glancing at her during the screening of the latest comedy film, saw that she was staring straight ahead while the tears poured down her face.

Lucy, her flatmate, was delighted to see her back, once she had recovered from the shock of wandering groggily into the kitchen at ten o'clock to find Darcy sitting at the tiny breakfast-bar, her hands clasped round a mug of coffee and an expression of utter despair in her eyes. Lucy, who had never seen such a look on Darcy's face before, put it down to jet-lag.

'We were all beginning to think you were never coming back,' she said, perching on the other stool when the first exclamations and explanations were over. 'Surely you haven't been stuck in the outback all this time?'

'Yes,' said Darcy, swirling her coffee round in her mug.

'Must have been a bit grim.' Lucy made a face. 'What was it like?'

What was it like? Darcy looked down into her coffee and realised that she would never be able to explain. How could Lucy understand what it was like to stand by the creek or sit on top of a fire-red dune? How could she begin to describe a light so sharp that it hurt the eyes, or stars so clear you could almost grasp them?

'It was beautiful,' was all she said.

Disappointed at Darcy's uncharacteristic lack of enthusiasm, Lucy left for a rehearsal soon afterwards. 'By the way,' she remembered, putting her head back round the front door on her way out, 'I've put any post in your room. An official-looking letter arrived just after you left, but I thought it was safest just to keep it here till you got back.'

Darcy sat on the bed and looked through the pile of letters without interest—a few notes from friends commiserating about Sebastian or the play's lack of success, several invitations, bank statements and credit-card bills which she left unopened and, at the bottom, a letter from Adelaide.

It was from the solicitors. Darcy unfolded the thick cream paper with a horrible sense of *déjà vu*. The last time she had picked up a letter like this from Uncle

Bill's desk, her whole world had fallen apart. The letterhead, the type, even the signature was the same.

Another, smaller envelope fell out as she unfolded the letter. Darcy turned it over, puzzled, then read the solicitor's profuse apologies for not having forwarded the enclosed letter from her uncle with his previous letter informing her of her inheritance. Slowly, Darcy laid it aside, and tore open the envelope, smoothing Uncle Bill's letter out on to her lap with shaking hands. It was written in his spidery hand.

My dear niece,

I have few regrets in life, but the greatest is that I did not swallow my pride and go back to England earlier. The knowledge that I had a warm and affectionate family has been a great comfort to me, and your letters in a time of trouble meant more than I can say. I leave you Bindaburra as a mark of my affection and gratitude.

Bindaburra does not belong only to me. Some years ago I was faced with the choice of selling the property entirely, or selling half of it to raise enough capital to carry on. I chose to sell half to a local man I had known and respected, but the contract we drew up did not prevent him from selling his share in turn to a man I considered to be dishonest and unprincipled. It was at this stage that I resolved to leave you Bindaburra, as I could not contemplate my property falling into his hands.

I was rescued from this unhappy partnership by Cooper Anderson, who cares for Bindaburra as much as I do. He has let me carry on as if the property were entirely mine, on the unwritten understanding that control would revert to him on my death. I owe him a debt of gratitude I can never repay. He deserves Bindaburra, but Bindaburra is all that I have to leave you. I know that you have your own life in London, and my hope is that you will let Cooper buy back my share from you. Please use the money to buy yourself something that you would like and that will remind you of me. I hope too that you will be able to come out to see Bindaburra for yourself. I know that Cooper would make you welcome. He is a fine man and I think you would like him.

Your very affectionate uncle, William Meadows.

Darcy's eyes were full of tears. His legal friend had obviously rewritten much of the letter and corrected his grammar, but she could still sense her great-uncle very strongly.

She had done Cooper a grave injustice. Uncle Bill had considered him a fine man, and she had more reason than most to know just how fine he was, and yet she had believed him capable of obsession and bullying and deceit. Cooper had deserved Bindaburra, just as Uncle Bill had said, but, more importantly, he had deserved her trust, and she had failed him.

Darcy buried her face in her hands and wept.

Why hadn't she waited a few days more before rushing off to Australia? Judging by the date on the solicitor's letter, it could only have arrived a day or so after she'd left. Things might have been so different if only she had read it before turning up at Bindaburra and behaving in the very last way Uncle Bill would have wanted her to. He would have been bitterly ashamed of her.

Later that day, Darcy sat down and wrote two letters of her own. The first was to the solicitors, the second to Cooper himself. It took her a long time to write. There was so much that she wanted to say, to unsay, but she couldn't find the words for any of it. She wrote in the end:

Dear Cooper,
  I have written to the solicitors today asking them to transfer my share of Bindaburra to you. Please do not send me any money. I know now that Uncle Bill did indeed mean you to have it. I have my memories of a very beautiful place, and that is enough for me. I know too that I was very wrong to accuse you of being anything other than kind and generous to him. I cannot tell you how much I regret the things I said.

When she read it back it sounded bald and inadequate, but what else could she say? Scrawling 'I'm sorry' hurriedly across the bottom, she signed her name and thrust the page into an envelope before she had time to change her mind. She couldn't tell Cooper how much she loved him still, not when she had taken that love and tossed it carelessly away. She kept remembering the last time she had seen him, the bitter contempt in his eyes just before he'd closed the bedroom door on her.

All she could do was hope that he might forgive her. If he loved her as he had said he did, surely he would at least read her letter and, when he saw how sorry she was, might he not write and ask her to come back to Bindaburra?

Feeling that she had done all she could, Darcy took the letters down to the post office and only when she

had dropped them into the box did she allow herself
to go home and sleep.

She had to force herself not to jump on the post
as it dropped through the door each day. Knowing
how long the mail sometimes sat at Muroonda before
anyone had time to collect it, she told herself that she
couldn't possibly even hope for a reply before three
weeks. It didn't stop her heart leaping every time she
heard the rattle of the letterbox.

Darcy's friends did everything they could to distract her. To please them, she tried to be cheerful, but
in theatres and pubs, restaurants and wine bars, surrounded by chatter and gossip, her mind would slide
inevitably back to the quiet creek at Bindaburra where
the only sounds were the cries of birds and Cooper's
footsteps along the veranda. She yearned for the space
and the light and the clear, starlit nights—and for
Cooper.

She missed him with a physical ache like a cramp
around her heart. At night, she would lie awake and
remember the way he used to touch her, and her body
would strum with need while the despair and the
longing clutched at her viciously.

Three weeks passed, four, six, seven, and Darcy
came to accept that Cooper wasn't going to write.
There would be no letter telling her everything would
be all right and urging her to get the next flight back
to Australia. He didn't love her enough to forgive her.
Perhaps he never had.

She had been wrong about his relationship with
Uncle Bill, but she might have been right in accusing
him of wanting Bindaburra more than he wanted her.
Now he had Bindaburra and he didn't need her any

more. Why couldn't she just accept that and get on with her life here?

When the letter came from the solicitors the next morning, the last faint hope was crushed. The transfer of her holdings in Bindaburra to Mr Anderson had been completed, they said. Mr Anderson had insisted on giving an extremely generous price for the land, and they had opened an account in her name while awaiting her instructions.

So this was the end. Bindaburra was no longer hers and the last link with Cooper was gone.

The sense of loss was overwhelming. Darcy stood staring numbly down at the letter, unable to believe that it was all over. She felt empty, bereft, panic-stricken at the thought of never being able to go back.

The cramped flat pressed around her, taunting her with memories of the wide, empty horizons and arching skies she had lost. Suddenly desperate to get out, Darcy pushed the letter in her pocket and let herself out of the flat. She began walking blindly down the street, not knowing where she was going, not caring, just needing to walk.

London was enjoying a belated burst of summer and the streets were full of sunshine. Darcy hardly noticed. The first terrible numbness was fading before an invigorating rush of anger. She was furious with Cooper for pretending to love her when all he had had to do was wait, furious with herself for carrying on hoping right to the end.

Without ever knowing quite how she got there, Darcy found herself at the gates of Battersea Park. The first thing she saw as she walked through was a wallaby watching her through the wire of an enclosure which held an odd assortment of small animals and birds. A mother was holding a fascinated child's hand and explaining about kangaroos and where they lived.

'What's Australia?' asked the little girl.

'It's a place, darling. It's a place a long, long way away from here.'

A place of dazzling light and huge skies, of stillness and silence and far horizons. Never had it seemed further away.

Darcy looked sympathetically back at the wallaby trapped behind the wire and wandered on around the lake. It was lunchtime. Office workers were lying on the grass, reading newspapers and eating sandwiches, ignoring the pigeons who strutted around them in search of crumbs.

There was an empty bench by the lake. Anger ebbing along with her energy, Darcy sat down. Immediately a grey squirrel started running round in circles by her feet, stopping every now and then to check whether she had noticed and was ready to throw him a titbit. It could hardly have picked a less responsive audience. Darcy didn't even see its attempts to show off. She was staring out across the lake and remembering the still surface of the creek, where there were parrots and pelicans instead of ducks and pigeons and only dry, dusty curls of bark instead of manicured green grass.

The loneliness and the longing crashed over her again then and the tears spilt down her cheeks. Darcy tried to brush them away, but it was hopeless, and a stranger had to pick that moment to come up and share the bench. Turning her face away, she groped desperately for a tissue.

A handkerchief appeared under her nose. 'Here, have this,' said Cooper's voice.

Darcy froze. Had she imagined it, or had that really been Cooper's voice? Slowly, very slowly, she turned.

Cooper was sitting beside her, still holding out the handkerchief. He wore no hat, but otherwise he looked exactly the same. His eyes, his mouth, the cool, angular planes of his face . . . all just as she had pictured so yearningly over the last seven weeks. Afraid that she might be hallucinating, Darcy squeezed her eyes shut, but when she opened them he was still there, watching her with a hard, anxious expression.

'How did you get here?' she whispered, not entirely convinced yet that he was real.

'I followed you. I was on my way to your house when I saw you marching off in the other direction,' Cooper explained when Darcy only stared. 'You didn't look as if you wanted to talk to anybody, and anyway I didn't think we could have a proper conversation in the street, so I followed you here.'

'I see,' said Darcy, who didn't see at all, but it didn't seem to matter. How many nights had she lain awake dreaming of what she would tell him if she ever saw him again? Now she couldn't think of anything to say, could only gaze at him and allow herself to believe the wonderful, glorious, miraculous fact that he was there at last.

'Here,' he said, offering her the handkerchief again. This time she took it and rubbed her face absently. 'Why were you crying?' he asked. 'Didn't you get the part?'

'What part?'

'The starring role you came back to audition for.'

Darcy looked back at the lake. It wasn't a lake really, it was just a big pond. 'There wasn't any starring role,' she said quietly.

She felt rather than saw the tension go out of him. 'It was just an excuse to leave?'

'Yes.'

The squirrel was trying out its act on Cooper, with no more success than before. Darcy struggled to grasp the reality of Cooper's sudden appearance after seven bleak weeks.

'Why have you come?' she burst out, swinging back to face him almost accusingly. 'You've got what you've always wanted!'

'No, I haven't.' Cooper shook his head. 'Not yet.'

'You needn't worry, I got the letter from the solicitors today.' Darcy pulled the crumpled envelope from her pocket and thrust it at him. 'Read that if you don't believe me. The transfer has gone through, so Bindaburra is all yours.'

'I know that,' said Cooper, ignoring the envelope. 'I rang the solicitors myself this morning to check.'

'I suppose you couldn't wait!'

'No,' he said. 'I couldn't. But do you know why?'

'I could make a good guess,' she said bitterly.

'It would be the wrong one, Darcy,' said Cooper in a quiet voice. 'Would you like to know the real reason why I was so impatient to know that Bindaburra belonged entirely to me?'

'All right.' Darcy mopped her eyes with the handkerchief. 'Why?'

'Because I knew that until it did you would never believe that *you* were all I've always wanted.'

There was a long silence. Darcy lowered the handkerchief. 'Would you say that again?' she whispered.

'I don't want Bindaburra if I can't have you, Darcy,' said Cooper softly. 'I never wanted your land. I just wanted you to stay at Bindaburra with me.'

Darcy's eyes were beginning to glow a deep, beautiful blue. 'You really *do* love me?' she asked huskily, and he slid his fingers through her soft hair.

'Darcy, how could you ever have doubted it?' he said, tightening his hands to pull her across the bench towards him for a kiss which left them both breathless and shaken. Darcy dissolved into him, the joy as sharp as pain as his mouth met hers at last, and the bitterness and the desolation sank beneath wave after wave of blissful relief.

The squirrel gave up in disgust and went to try his luck with a couple of secretaries who were sitting on the next bench and trying not to watch enviously.

'Now do you believe that I love you?' Cooper mumbled into her hair.

'Oh, yes,' sighed Darcy, kissing his throat.

'Aren't you going to tell me that you love me too?'

'But you know that!'

'How was I supposed to know it when you told me you wanted to go home and be an actress again?' he asked, not unreasonably.

'Oh, Cooper, will you ever forgive me for being so stupid?' Darcy buried herself against him, clinging to his strong, solid body. 'I was so confused and miserable. When I found that letter from Uncle Bill's solicitor, I didn't know what to think. I couldn't bear the thought that it might be about you, but it just talked about Uncle Bill's partner, and as far as I knew you were the only partner he'd ever had.'

'I thought Melanie told you about her father?' said Cooper, trying to be stern but spoiling the effect by putting his arm around her and holding her close.

'She did, and I was so relieved that it might be him after all, but then she started talking about how you were only interested in getting Bindaburra, and I started remembering things you said to me...' Darcy trailed off. Now that she was safe in his arms again, she was hardly able to believe that she could have considered for a moment that Cooper might not love her. 'And you didn't make me feel any better by ignoring me all evening and flirting with all those women who kept throwing themselves at you,' she added defensively.

'Well, if we're going to talk about *flirting*...! What were you doing all evening?'

'I just wanted you to notice me,' confessed Darcy, curling her fingers into his palm. 'I wanted you to drag me away and convince me that you loved me for myself, but you didn't seem to care what I did. That was when I thought Melanie must be right after all.'

'I was just jealous,' said Cooper. 'You'd been behaving so strangely that I thought you'd begun to get bored with Bindaburra, and when you made such a show of enjoying the party it seemed as if you were remembering the sort of life you'd had before. I don't think I was even surprised when you said you wanted to go home. And then when you accused me of bullying Bill... well, for a time I was so angry, I thought *I* wanted you to go too.'

'I'm sorry,' she said inadequately. 'I should have trusted you, but I hated the thought of Uncle Bill being distressed. Was it Melanie's father after all?'

'No, Reg Collins is an honest man. He didn't go into partnership with Bill until after Melanie had married Jed, so any story she told you about me persuing her in hope of Bindaburra was sheer spite. She certainly knew that I wanted to get the property back into the family one day, but that was common knowledge in the area. Bill and my father didn't talk because of it, so when times got hard he accepted Reg's offer for a half-share instead of mine—and lived to regret it. He and Reg got on well enough as partners, but a year or so later Reg made his share over to Jed and Melanie.

'That's when the trouble began. Jed thought he would find oil on Bindaburra. He wasn't interested in investing in the land; he wanted to exploit it, and he didn't intend to let Bill stand in his way. Bill could stand up for himself, of course, but he felt that he was getting old and the constant arguments wore him down. That was one of the reasons he went to England. Bindaburra didn't seem to be the same place any more and I think he was wondering whether to give up. It was something you said that made him decide to go home and fight.'

Darcy sat up in astonishment. 'Something *I* said?'

'Apparently you were telling him about acting. You said that it wasn't easy, but that you thought life should be about doing what you loved, not regretting what you *weren't* doing.' Cooper smiled down at her and smoothed a stray lock of hair away from her face. 'Bill was very impressed by the way you threw your heart into whatever you were doing. You reminded him of how much Bindaburra meant to him, and when he got back he came to see me.'

'I thought he wasn't on speaking terms with the Andersons?'

'He wasn't, or hadn't been with my father, anyway. It must have cost him a lot to come and tell me that he'd made a mistake in not accepting my offer. At least he knew that I would care for Bindaburra as he had done and not turn it into a vast oil field.'

'How did you get rid of Jed?'

'Like all bullies, he's a coward at heart. I simply went to see him and told him that I was going into partnership with Bill and that he would find me much more difficult to deal with if he persisted in his attempts at intimidation. I offered him a fair price for his share and suggested that he would do better to cut his losses and try for his oil somewhere else.'

'You must have done more than that!'

Cooper smiled grimly. 'Let's just say that I managed to convince Jed that it would be in his own best interests,' he said, and Darcy thought that Jed had probably made a very wise decision in doing exactly what Cooper wanted.

'Didn't he mind?'

'Oh, he minded all right,' said Cooper laconically. 'He's never forgiven me for what he thinks of as a humiliation, and he never misses a chance to try and stir trouble if he can. That's why he would have made such a fuss of you. He'd only need to look at you to guess how I might feel about you, and the chance to score off me again would have been irresistible.'

'But why would Melanie lie to me about you? You hadn't humiliated her. If anything, it was the other way round.'

He shrugged. 'I don't think it ever occurred to Melanie that I wouldn't still be hopelessly in love with her. I was supposed to be inconsolable, and she didn't like the fact that instead of languishing for her as she'd imagined I'd fallen in love with you. She didn't want me herself, but she was determined that no one else was going to have me. She thought that all she had to do was offer herself to me again and I would fall down on my knees with gratitude,' he went on, shaking his head as if still incredulous at the memory. 'She didn't like it when I told her exactly what I thought of her offer.'

Darcy remembered the scene she had witnessed at the party, and Melanie's twisted face as she had turned away from Cooper. 'You mean she'd wanted to persuade me to leave so that she could have you herself?'

'Partly, but mainly because Melanie never liked any competition. She would have been jealous of you even if you'd had nothing to do with me, just because of the way you looked.'

'I can't imagine Melanie being jealous of anyone's looks,' said Darcy in surprise. 'Especially not mine!'

Cooper smiled and traced his thumb down her cheek. 'Her features might be perfect, but next to you she looked cold and colourless. She knew that if I'd fallen in love with someone so different it meant that I'd never really been in love with her at all, and she didn't like it. It's not surprising they both did their best to make trouble for us. Melanie didn't want to see you as my wife, and Jed didn't want to see me settled at Bindaburra at last.'

'It looks as if they're both in for a disappointment, then, doesn't it?' said Darcy, and kissed his cheek.

'Does that mean you'll marry me and come back to Bindaburra?' Cooper asked, his grey eyes alight with such a look of love that Darcy felt herself melt into his arms.

'Try stopping me,' she said. It was a longer kiss this time, warm and sweet with the promise of the years to come. 'I wonder if this is what Uncle Bill had in mind when he said that he hoped I'd go out to Bindaburra?' mumbled Darcy happily when she could. 'He said he thought I would like you!'

'I wouldn't have put it past him to try a bit of matchmaking,' said Cooper with another grin. 'I used to get sick of hearing about you. We'd agreed that Bill would stay at Bindaburra and run the property on his own for as long as he wanted, but I used to go over and have a chat sometimes. I wanted to hear about the cattle, but he just wanted to talk about this English girl who I thought sounded unbearable. I couldn't understand why anyone as down-to-earth as Bill would have been taken in by you, and then you came...' He smiled down into Darcy's shining eyes. 'You know the rest! I took one look into those beautiful blue eyes and I was a lost man!'

'At least we know he would have approved,' she said in contentment.

Cooper reached into his pocket. 'I think he would have approved of your wearing this, too,' he said, and opened his hand to show the ring Uncle Bill had bought for Violet all those years ago. He had had it cleaned, and the diamonds glinted against the gold in the sunlight. 'I brought it with me, just in case,' he said. 'It's yours anyway, but I thought you might like to have this one, since it was Bill who brought us together.' He paused and looked down into her face. 'I could buy you a ring of your own if you'd prefer.'

'No.' Darcy shook her head. 'I'd rather have this one, for Uncle Bill. He would have liked to think of his ring being worn at last. You can buy me a wedding-ring,' she promised, holding out her hand so that Cooper could slide the ring on to her finger.

'And a new cooker,' he said, and kissed her again.

Darcy sighed with sheer happiness as she emerged and leant her head against his shoulder, twisting her hand so that the diamonds flashed joyfully on her finger. 'I wish we hadn't wasted so much time together,' she said. 'You've no idea how miserable I've been without you.'

'Haven't I?' Cooper tipped her face back up to his. 'What do you think it was like for me to come back to the homestead that day and find that you'd gone after all? It was so cold and quiet without you. I used to sit on the veranda and feel the memory of you echoing around me. I kept thinking I heard your laugh, or caught sight of you out of the corner of my eye, and sometimes I'd wake at night and imagine that I could feel you breathing beside me. Then I'd turn over and reach out for you, and remember that you weren't there.'

Darcy's eyes were starry with tears. 'It's been the same for me. I've been *aching* for you,' she said, and they kissed to banish those terrible memories. 'Why didn't you come sooner?' she murmured at last. 'Didn't you get my letter?'

'Yes, and wore it out with reading it over and over again.' Cooper shifted his arm to hold her more comfortably. 'I thought about jumping on a plane there and then, but you didn't say anything about loving me in your letter. I decided I would wait until your share had been transferred completely to me so that you wouldn't have any grounds for thinking I wanted you for anything other than yourself.' He paused and kissed her hair. 'I thought it would give you a chance too to decide what you really wanted. If you'd got the part you said you were going to audition for, you might have decided to concentrate on your career after all. I was always conscious that I didn't have much to offer you compared to the life you might have here, and I could only hope that you might decide that you wanted me and Bindaburra after all.'

'I decided that a long time ago,' said Darcy. 'I understood why you thought we shouldn't get married immediately before, but now I know how desperately I need you we don't have to wait any longer, do we?'

'No, I think we've both had quite long enough to think about it,' Cooper agreed. 'Now that I've got you, I'm not letting you go again.'

'And you don't mind having such a useless wife?' she teased him, remembering how unimpressed he had been when he'd first met her.

'Who said you were useless?' Cooper pretended to sound outraged. 'No one burns a steak quite like you do. We've all missed that distinctive taste of carbon!' His eyes grew serious. 'You're not useless, Darcy. You never have been. You made a house a home, and you made me happy. Nothing could be more useful than that!'

'You're sure you don't want me to do a quick cooking course?'

'No, I don't want you to change at all.' Laughter glimmered in the grey eyes again. 'If you learn to cook, I might have to learn to get in touch with my emotions like Sebastian!'

Darcy laughed. 'I love your emotions just the way they are,' she promised him.

'What about your acting?' asked Cooper when he had kissed her once more. 'The only role I can offer you in my life is as partner and wife.'

She pretended to consider. 'How long does the production last?'

'Forever,' he said, smiling.

'And would I have the starring role?'

'Definitely.'

Darcy sighed happily. 'It sounds the perfect part for me,' she said.

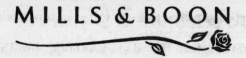

MILLS & BOON

Next Month's Romances

Each month you can choose from a wide variety of romance with Mills & Boon. Below are the new titles to look out for next month.

THE SHINING OF LOVE	Emma Darcy
A BRIEF ENCOUNTER	Catherine George
SECRET OBSESSION	Charlotte Lamb
A VERY SECRET AFFAIR	Miranda Lee
DEAREST LOVE	Betty Neels
THE WEDDING EFFECT	Sophie Weston
UNWELCOME INVADER	Angela Devine
UNTOUCHED	Sandra Field
THIEF OF HEARTS	Natalie Fox
FIRE AND SPICE	Karen van der Zee
JUNGLE FEVER	Jennifer Taylor
BEYOND ALL REASON	Cathy Williams
FOREVER ISN'T LONG ENOUGH	Val Daniels
TRIUMPH OF LOVE	Barbara McMahon
IRRESISTIBLE ATTRACTION	Alison Kelly
FREE TO LOVE	Alison York

To celebrate 10 years of Temptation we are giving away a host of tempting prizes...

All you have to do is complete the wordsearch puzzle below and send it to us by 31 May 1995.

The first 10 correct entries drawn from the bag will each win 12 month's free supply of exciting Temptation books (4 books every month with a total annual value of around £100).

The second 10 correct entries drawn will each win a 200g box of _Thorntons_ Temptations chocolates.

I	F	G	N	I	T	I	C	X	E
A	O	X	O	C	A	I	N	S	S
N	O	I	T	A	T	P	M	E	T
N	B	V	E	N	R	Y	N	X	E
I	R	O	A	M	A	S	N	Y	R
V	C	M	T	I	U	N	N	F	U
E	O	H	U	O	T	M	V	E	T
R	N	X	U	R	E	Y	S	I	N
S	L	S	M	A	N	F	L	Y	E
A	T	O	N	U	T	R	X	L	V
R	U	O	M	U	H	I	A	A	D
Y	W	D	Y	O	F	I	M	K	A

TEMPTATION   ROMANTIC
SEXY   SENSUOUS
FUN   ADVENTURE
EXCITING   HUMOUR
TENTH   ANNIVERSARY

→ PLEASE TURN OVER FOR ENTRY DETAILS

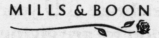

MILLS & BOON

HOW TO ENTER

All the words listed overleaf below the wordsearch puzzle, are hidden in the grid. You can find them by reading the letters forward, backwards, up and down, or diagonally. When you find a word, circle it or put a line through it.

Don't forget to fill in your name and address in the space below then put this page in an envelope and post it today (you don't need a stamp). Closing date 31st May 1995.

Temptation Wordsearch,
FREEPOST,
P.O. Box 344,
Croydon,
Surrey
CR9 9EL

COMP395

Are you a Reader Service Subscriber?   Yes ☐ No ☐

Ms/Mrs/Miss/Mr _____

Address _____

_____

_____ Postcode _____